HER FOOLISH HEART

At twenty-nine, Miss Georgina Goring was wise enough to know how foolish her youthful niece Susan was to fall in love with Lord Randal Kenyon, who had successfully evaded society's most accomplished husband-hunters.

Georgina was wise enough to help Susan counter the competition of Marianne MacClain, who already had a London season of experience behind her lovely person to sharpen her seductive skills.

But though Georgina had reached the age of sufficient wisdom to aid Susan, she soon discovered how far from wise her own heart was in the presence of this lord whom too many other ladies wanted for her to even dream of winning. . . .

The Irresolute Rivals

THE IRRESOLUTE RIVALS

◆◆◆ by ◆◆◆

Jane Ashford

A SIGNET BOOK

NEW AMERICAN LIBRARY

Copyright © 1985 by Jane LeCompte

SIGNET, SIGNET CLASSIC, MENTOR, PLUME, MERIDIAN and NAL BOOKS
are published by New American Library,
1633 Broadway, New York, New York 10019

First Printing, February, 1985

1 2 3 4 5 6 7 8 9

PRINTED IN THE UNITED STATES OF AMERICA

1

"It really does look *splendid*, does it not?" said eighteen-year-old Susan Wyndham, turning before the long glass to admire the flowing line of her pale green ball gown.

"Splendid," agreed her second cousin Georgina Goring, her twinkling gray eyes the only sign that this was at least the sixth time she had done so.

"I told you the ruffle at the hem would become me." Susan whirled to make the skirt bell out. "I am so glad I convinced the dressmaker to copy that pattern from *La Belle Assemblée*, in spite of her *ridiculous* objections. I do want to look stunning for my first ball."

Georgina, her expression wry as she thought of the turn-up with the dressmaker, admitted to herself that Susan could hardly have looked ill. Her much younger cousin was exquisitely pretty, and had been since Georgina first met her at the age of six. Her hair was glowing red and her eyes sparkling green. She had the delicate figure of a Dresden shepherd-ess and the endurance of a navvy. If only, thought Georgina, her character was as perfect as her face, I shouldn't worry for a moment. She sighed softly. For Georgina, at the relatively young age of twenty-nine, had been put in charge of Susan's debut in society.

Susan's mother was fully occupied at home with a brood of younger children—the result of her second marriage—and though there was great love between Anabel and her spirited daughter, the former was a confirmed country dweller and only too glad to delegate her responsibility. Susan's grandmother, Lady Sybil Goring, had happily taken it on, inviting the girl to her London town house and promising a variety of treats, but she had not been well lately, and a short visit by Georgina had been prolonged to allow Lady Goring to recover completely before resuming her social duties.

Georgina sighed again. Aunt Sybil *believed* herself within a few days of robust health, but the doctor's opinion was far different. It had been clear to Georgina for some time that she would be Susan's chief guide through the shoals of the opening Season. And this was doubly ironic—first because Georgina's own debut had been far from auspicious, and second because she was not at all certain she could control her young cousin, or even influence her.

Almost from birth, Susan Wyndham had been possessed of a lightning-quick, hot temper. It had made her a difficult child, and it showed small sign of moderation, in Georgina's opinion, with the passage of years. The trouble with the dressmaker was only one example. Georgina had mediated a series of disputes since the girl's arrival less than two weeks ago. In all other ways, Susan was charming, and her anger dissipated rapidly and completely, often leaving her sheepish and apologetic. But in the first white heat of combat, she was formidable, despite her youth, and Georgina did not relish the prospect of chaperoning her among the *haut ton*.

There were many who would revel in rousing

Susan, once her character was known, to discover how far she would go when angry, and Georgina shuddered to think of the consequences. Thus, her responsibility weighed heavily on her, obscuring any enjoyment she might have anticipated from the Season.

Of course, she expected little in any case. Georgina was more at home in a country town than in a drawing room. She had learned something of the *ton*'s rituals during her own come-out ten years before, but her performance of them had been no more than adequate. She had arrived in London a bookish, overplump, and somewhat sullen young girl, resentful of the necessity to "come out," and though she had changed a great deal during those weeks, and even more in the years that followed, she was no more fond of town life. She wished, as she had many times in the last few days, that she could return to her quiet home. Though Papa had died four years ago, and she missed him, Georgina was content with her novels, her household tasks, and the round of visits and entertainments of country neighbors. That was the sort of society she loved, and in which she shone—a close-knit group of friends who shared both interests and experiences. Faced with Susan Wyndham, Georgina felt alarmingly like her clumsy young self, helpless in the grip of events and nearly certain the outcome would be disaster.

"Georgina," said Susan, her tone making it clear that she had spoken more than once. "What is the matter with you?"

Her cousin looked up as if startled. "Nothing."

Susan surveyed her with pursed lips, deploring yet again Georgina's woolly-headedness. She did not understand how Georgina managed to get through a day without falling into the fire or walking in front of a moving carriage. Half the time when one spoke to her, she didn't hear, and when she did, the answers she gave were usually nonsensical. Only yesterday, as they had been walking along Bond Street among the smartest shops, when Susan had pointed out a ravishing bonnet, Georgina had answered, "She is his sister, I think, not his wife," and it had turned out she was talking about a pair of complete strangers and paying no heed to Susan at all. Indeed, she often seemed oblivious of Susan, a trait which that self-absorbed young lady found incomprehensible. How unfortunate it was that Grandmama should be ill just now, Susan thought, not for the first time: for her own sake, of course, and also for Susan's. Georgina was a far less promising chaperon. Grandmama knew everyone and could have pointed out the notables and told their histories. Georgina would know hardly anyone here. It was vastly irritating, and it might even, she worried, interfere with Susan's unwavering ambition to become a celebrated belle. Lady Goring was the picture of fashionable elegance, and widely respected; all would notice her cherished granddaughter. But Georgina was unfashionable; there could be no two opinions about that.

There was nothing actually wrong with her appearance. She was of medium height, taller than Susan, and had a pleasing fine-boned frame. Her hair was a delicate pale blond and curled naturally into tendrils about her head, though it was *not* dressed in the latest mode, Susan thought. Her thickly lashed gray eyes were very striking, dominating an oval face with a straight nose and beautifully etched mouth above a determined chin. And Susan freely admitted that Georgina had a way of moving, or turning her head slowly, that took one suddenly aback and revised one's opinion of her abruptly. At such times, there was an immense dignity and elegance in her carriage. If only she would make a push, lamented Susan silently, she could be the height of fashion. But no hint of Susan's seemed to reach her. Georgina went on wearing sadly simple gowns in the dullest colors. Her ball gown was a glaring example; it was of a washed-out rose and devoid of the simplest trim— not a ruffle or a knot of ribbon embellished its flow to the tips of Georgina's kid slippers. How could she expect to be distinguished in a garment such as *that*? wondered Susan with irritation.

She raised her eyes, met Georgina's gray ones, and had the uneasy feeling that her cousin knew exactly what she had been thinking. That was another trouble with Georgina. She saw through one in a way that Grandmama never did.

The corners of Georgina's mouth turned up a little, but she suppressed her smile. She was indeed fully aware of Susan's opinion of her clothes. But she disliked disputes, particularly with hot-tempered opponents, and she was too kind to point out that Susan's idea of elegance was rudimentary. Georgina rather prided herself on her taste, but the effect was rather too subtle for a girl fresh from the schoolroom, and of a radically different temperament and coloring. "We should be going," said Georgina. "The carriage is probably waiting."

"Oh yes," answered Susan, forgetting all else in her excitement over the coming ball. "I'm ready."

Smiling, Georgina indicated her wrap, and the two walked downstairs side by side, each contemplating the evening ahead with rather different emotions.

Though the ball was one of the first events of the

Season, it was also expected to be among the most brilliant. The Duchess of Millshire's eldest daughter was making her debut, and she was to be introduced with the greatest possible fanfare. The *ton* had been buzzing for weeks about the duchess's vast preparations, and none of the leading lights would be absent tonight. Indeed, Susan and Georgina were forced to wait nearly twenty minutes in Lady Goring's town carriage before the coachman could maneuver through the press of vehicles and deposit them at the pillared doorway. The delay raised Susan's impatience to fever pitch, and gave Georgina a sinking sensation, so that neither was at her best when they climbed the three steps and were admitted to the house by a liveried footman.

"Oh, do come on," said Susan, when Georgina was a bit slow in removing her wrap. "The dancing has probably started long since. We are missing everything!"

"I imagine, rather, that Lady Helen is still greeting guests with her mother," replied Georgina calmly, but she relinquished her cloak and started up the stairs.

All of the family was indeed still at their summit, and Susan looked a little less sulky as they greeted their hosts and conveyed Lady Goring's regrets. And when they moved on into the ballroom, her annoyance faded in wide-eyed admiration of the decoration, for the duchess had spared nothing in decking her house for the occasion.

"Look there," exclaimed Susan as they walked. "That is a *fountain* in the corner, amongst those roses, and it is running!"

"I see it." Georgina was smiling.

Her cousin looked back. "You are laughing at me."

"I am not."

"You were. I suppose I sound hopelessly countrified. I must—"

"Look out," interrupted Georgina, who had noticed a group of guests approaching them from the side. Like Susan, they were engrossed in conversation.

But it was too late. Susan did not check, and the others had not seen. In the next moment, the girl had collided with a much taller young woman, and the two were forced to hang on to one another to keep from falling.

"I beg your pardon," began Susan.

"I'm sorry, I wasn't looking," said the other.

Then both fell abruptly silent and moved apart, staring. For, amazingly, they wore the same gown, down to the flouncing at the hem. The fabrics were a little different, but as the color was pale green, this scarcely signified. At first glance, the garments appeared identical.

And this coincidence was made more startling by a superficial resemblance between the two girls. Both had vivid red hair and pale skin; both were strikingly lovely. And though the stranger's statuesque form and height contrasted strongly with Susan's delicacy, the difference merely accentuated the sartorial contretemps. The silence spread for quite five yards around them as people noticed the unusual tableau.

Georgina, seeing Susan's cheeks flame, opened her mouth to say something, anything, to ease the situation. But Susan was before her. "How dare you?" she said.

"What?" The taller girl had been looking slightly amused as well as disconcerted, but Susan's tone made her raise her eyebrows.

"Copy my gown," Susan hissed. As usual, her anger made her irrational. When it faded, she might well admit that this embarrassing misfortune was her own fault—for anyone might copy a fashion plate, after all. But just now she could see only the ruin of her plans to dazzle the *ton* and establish herself in society. She would be laughed at rather than admired. And the intolerable fact that this woman had her coloring, while a striking contrast in every other respect, only fed Susan's fury by spotlighting all the traits she had ever deplored in herself—her small stature, her tendency to fragility instead of curves, and the irritating air of innocence her features seemed to convey, when she wished to appear worldly and sophisticated. It was beyond bearing. At that moment, Susan would gladly have slapped the other's face.

"If we are to talk of copying," she replied, still seeming a bit amused through her annoyance, "*I* have had this dress since last Season. So you are the imitator." The newcomer could not resist this gibe, for the encounter had made her feel like a great clumsy giant confronting her image in miniature, and the sensation was far from pleasant. Though she could see the humor of the situation, its public character destroyed her impulse to laugh.

Susan's flush intensified, and her hands clenched at her sides. Any of her family would have quailed at these unmistakable signs.

"Isn't this too funny?" interjected Georgina, her voice sounding unnatural in her own ears. "I don't know when I've been so diverted." This was a feeble attempt, she knew, but something had to be done before Susan exposed herself before the whole of society.

"I should say, rather, exquisitely original," responded a deep baritone of such compelling magnetism that all three women turned instinctively. The man standing behind Georgina had not been part of either colliding group. He was also immediately identifiable to all but Susan. Even Georgina, whose knowledge of London society was small, could not mistake Randal Kenyon, Baron Ellerton. His physical appearance alone was distinctive. Tall, his well-formed person enhanced by various fashionable athletic pursuits, he radiated power and competence. And he was strikingly handsome as well, with deep chestnut hair and vivid blue eyes that seemed to take note of everything that passed before them. Indeed it was these eyes that transfixed the three women now; they were sparkling with intelligence and understanding of their dilemma, and with an amusement that somehow did not offend. "However did you conceive such a stunning effect?" he added, suppressing a smile at their patent amazement. "You have certainly made a hit. I congratulate you."

Susan gazed up at him, her anger forgotten in astonishment and confusion. The other girl smiled slightly, her own amusement returning. Georgina simply stared. Her low opinion of the *haut ton* gave this intervention the quality of miracle. Why, she wondered silently, should one of the leaders of society exert himself on their behalf? For even she had heard of Baron Ellerton's vast fortune, his unfailing elegance, and his political influence. She could see for herself that he epitomized the Corinthian, his evening dress severely perfect, his manner supremely assured. Yet he had taken it upon himself to save a situation that was threatening to rouse a storm of malicious laughter. Georgina defined the *ton* by its malice; what could the man be about?

"I hope you'll pardon my intrusion," he went on, blue eyes dancing at their expressions. "I could not resist complimenting you on your refreshing jest. Many women would have feared to try such a game, yet it is just the sort of thing we need. Do you know that there are women, and men too, who would be livid to meet another in the same ensemble."

"No, Baron Ellerton!" exclaimed the tall girl in mock astonishment.

"I assure you." They exchanged a smile. "At least, Lady Marianne, I am not guilty of pushing in where I am wholly unknown. Will you introduce me to your friends?"

"Er, Baron Ellerton, this is . . ." Lady Marianne turned to the others, perplexed. The baron's eyes twinkled anew.

But Georgina was too grateful to feel embarrassment. "Georgina Goring," she said. "And this is my cousin Miss Susan Wyndham."

Ellerton bowed slightly. "I have not seen you in town before, I think." And as he got a full view of Georgina for the first time, his manner shifted slightly. This was no silly chit, nor even a sensible girl, like Lady Marianne. Baron Ellerton instantly took in the distinctive character of Georgina's gown and expression, and smiled in appreciation.

"No, we have come for the Season." Georgina responded automatically to his smile. She could see no mockery in it.

"I don't understand," declared Susan, her tone indicating that she was fully prepared to resume hostilities.

Georgina hastened to reply, "Lord Ellerton perceived your joke at once, Susan. He saw that you and, er, Lady Marianne had devised a scheme to amuse everyone. I'm certain they have all noticed by this time how clever you were." She put heavy emphasis on this last phrase, trying to convey a great deal more in her look.

Susan gazed around the ballroom appraisingly. She had feared being laughed at, but if these Londoners thought she had done it on purpose . . . She contemplated this prospect for a moment. She was quite eager to be *noticed*, as long as the scrutiny was favorable.

Three pairs of eyes watched the shift of emotion so visible on Susan's face—Georgina anxiously, Lady Marianne quizzically, and Baron Ellerton biting his lower lip to keep from laughing.

Susan took a deep breath. "Yes, well, it was a good joke, wasn't it?"

Georgina could not restrain an audible sigh of relief.

"Capital," agreed Lady Marianne, then laughed.

"I can see that you two young women are very enterprising," added the baron. "You will be a definite asset to society." He glanced at Georgina as if to share a joke with her.

Susan looked up, truly seeing him for the first time now that her rage had dissipated, blinked, and looked again. His intense attractiveness and air of fashion seemed to register all at once, and she took another breath.

"And now, if you will excuse me," he said. "I have promised to open the dancing, and I believe they are waiting for me." With another small bow, he turned away. All three women watched him approach their hosts and lead the daughter of the house onto the floor to open the ball.

"What a complete hand he is," murmured Lady Marianne.

This brought Susan swinging around again. "Who is he?"

"Randal Kenyon, Baron Ellerton, one of the acknowledged leaders of the *ton*," she replied. "And a true gentleman, if this was any measure of his customary behavior. People will ask him about the incident, you know, and what he says will be taken up and repeated."

Georgina nodded, her gratitude welling up again. How would she have managed to smooth things over, she wondered, without his help?

"You mean, if he says we did it on purpose, everyone will believe him?" asked Susan.

"They will," answered Lady Marianne, "as they never would have if *we* said it." She smiled again. "And so, since we are to be talked of as great friends, perhaps we should become better acquainted. My name is Marianne MacClain. This is the start of my second Season in town."

"It is my first," responded Susan a bit grudgingly. She had not gotten over her envy of the other's poise.

"Well, you have made a fine start. It is not every newcomer who is noticed by Ellerton. I daresay you will be showered with invitations after this."

Susan turned to look at the baron once again, with this delightful prospect filling her head. He really was the handsomest man she had ever seen, and evidently a great catch. "Is he married?" Marianne shook her head. Susan smiled a little, then frowned as a dreadful suspicion entered her mind. "*You* are well acquainted with Lord Ellerton?" she asked.

Lady Marianne was also watching the dancers. "Not particularly. But I should *not* object to furthering my acquaintance."

"He helped *me*," snapped Susan, relieved.

"I beg your pardon?"

"Well, it must have been me. *You* were here last Season; he might have spoken to you anytime." Her tone implied that Lady Marianne had practically been left on the shelf.

"Susan!" said Georgina.

But Lady Marianne was smiling. "I had certain, er, other concerns last year."

"Marianne MacClain," gasped Georgina involuntarily. "You refused Lord Robert Devere!"

The other raised her russet eyebrows.

"Oh, I beg your pardon," said Georgina. "My aunt wrote me about it. I thought I had heard your name, and it suddenly came to me. . . ." She trailed off, once again conscious of her clumsiness with strangers.

"It doesn't matter. It is true, after all."

"Who is Lord Robert Devere?" asked Susan sharply.

Marianne looked around, then nodded toward the far corner of the ballroom. "There he is."

Susan looked, and saw a man as fashionable as Ellerton, though somewhat older and not, she thought, nearly so handsome. But it infuriated her that this confident girl should have actually received an offer from such a polished-looking nobleman, and rejected it! She felt bested again, a thing she hated above all else. "I don't see how that signifies," she said, tossing her head. "Lord Ellerton was clearly coming to my rescue." She looked at him again, calculating.

"I imagine he was simply amusing himself," corrected Marianne. "He is reputed to love oddities." She too directed a speculative gaze at the dance floor. "But he *was* very kind."

"To *me*," insisted Susan.

Marianne met her smoldering eyes, and her lips

curved upward. "Well, we shall see about that, shan't we?"

Susan did not look away. For a long moment they faced one another like duelists. Then Susan nodded once abruptly. "Yes. We shall." And without taking leave, she turned and walked toward the row of gilt chairs against the wall.

"Oh, dear," murmured Georgina. She looked from Susan to Marianne. "I beg your pardon. She did not mean . . ." She stopped, aware that Susan had meant various rude things.

Marianne MacClain laughed. "It doesn't matter. I know precisely how she feels. I daresay we shall really be great friends in the end, as Lord Ellerton has christened us."

Georgina looked doubtful. "I hope so."

A young man came up then, full of reproaches. "Lady Marianne! I have been searching everywhere. You promised me the first set."

With a smile and nod to Georgina, she allowed him to lead her away. Georgina turned to follow her cousin, a worried line remaining between her pale brows.

2

Lady Marianne MacClain spent the first part of the next morning alone in the drawing room of her family's town house wishing for callers. She was not a great reader, or indeed fond of any sedentary pursuits, and the lack of company soon began to wear on her patience. A year ago, such solitude would have been most unusual. Marianne could have been certain of the companionship of her mother and confident that her brother would appear at some time during the day. But both of these had married recently, her mother after a long widowhood, and now each was engrossed in personal concerns. Her brother Ian, Earl of Cairnyllan, was abroad visiting his new wife's father, the Duke of Morland, and her mother seemed to have become a different person since her own wedding to a long-ago suitor. Marianne understood, and applauded, her mother's efforts to erase memories of her first, unhappy match, but it was unsettling to see one's mother behaving like a girl newly married. Though they still lived in the same house, Marianne often felt as if they actually had separate establishments. And there were moments when she came near to resenting her new stepfather, Sir Thomas Bentham, though she in fact liked him very much.

Thus, the sounds of an arrival in the front hall below caused Marianne to jump up from her chair and run to the landing, straining to hear the exchange taking place at the door.

"I'm not certain Lady Marianne is in either," the butler was saying in the tone he reserved for doubtful callers.

"You mean everyone's out?" responded a youthful male voice. "Dash it, they had my letter a week ago."

The voice was unfamiliar. Marianne frowned as she tried to place it.

"Lady Bentham must have left instructions," insisted the visitor.

"Not to my knowledge, sir." But the butler sounded less discouraging.

"She and my cousin settled it all between them." The visitor sounded aggrieved. "I know no one in London. What am I to do? Kick up my heels in the street until Lady Bentham comes home?"

"If you will wait in the library, I will make inquiries."

The young man agreed reluctantly, and Marianne retreated to the drawing room as she heard the butler coming upstairs. In another moment he appeared. "I beg pardon, Lady Marianne, but a young gentleman has called. Or perhaps I should say, arrived. It seems that he is to stay with us." Hobbs looked reproachful. "I was not informed, or I should, of course, have ordered a room prepared."

"I don't know anything about it either, Hobbs." Marianne was intrigued. "Who is he?"

"His name is Brinmore, my lady."

She shook her head, perplexed. "I don't know anyone named Brinmore."

"He claims that Lady Bentham has corresponded with his cousin."

Since Marianne had overhead this, she was already puzzling over the connection. But she could not recall any mention of this man, or his family. It was an engaging mystery. "I suppose Mama forgot to tell me. She is . . . very busy lately." The butler ventured a commiserating look. Lady Bentham had always been gentle and absentminded rather than incisive, but since her marriage she seemed almost scatterbrained. "You had better bring him to me," concluded Marianne, concealing her pleasure in this unlooked-for development. "I will find out what it is all about."

Hobbs looked doubtful. "Shall I send for your maid, my lady?"

"I don't think this young man can be dangerous. But if Mama comes in, send her up at once."

The butler hesitated, not quite approving this decision, then turned away. "Very well, my lady."

Marianne couldn't help grinning at his back, stiff with offended propriety. If their stuffy London butler, recently added to the household, had any notion how she had grown up in Scotland, wholly unsupervised, he would no doubt expire from shock. Though she loved London and the amusements of the *haut ton*, its restrictions had been difficult for Marianne at first. Only her brother had ever tried to curb her before they left home, and him she had resisted with all her strength, rightly concluding that the notorious excesses of their father had made Ian too strict. It had required personal experience, along with the far more understanding and tactful guidance of the woman who had later become Ian's wife, to show Marianne that certain restraints were necessary, and even desirable. She had come close to making a number of mistakes, but Marianne was remarkably levelheaded, as well as intelligent, and she had learned quickly and well. This Season would be far calmer than last.

A reminiscent smile curved her lips; what rows she and Ian had had. If anyone had told her that she would actually miss them . . . She shook her head.

Thus, the visitor entered the drawing room to find a very beautiful girl smiling pensively at the carpet. He was momentarily transfixed. Though liking to think himself at ease in any situation, Mr. Brinmore was in fact not yet one-and-twenty, and this was his first visit to the metropolis. Moreover, his dealings with the fair sex had not so far included a girl as lovely and fashionable as Lady Marianne MacClain. He swallowed, very conscious of her status as daughter and sister of an earl. "Er, hello."

Marianne started, brought back from a great distance. "Oh, I beg your pardon. How do you do? Come in." He moved a bit further into the room. "I am Marianne MacClain, you know. Hobbs tells me you have come to stay with us?"

Her tone was perfectly amiable, but Brinmore flushed. "I understood it was all settled, but no one here seems to know anything about it. I don't know quite what—"

"I think you had best tell me the whole story," interrupted Marianne, seeing his discomfort. "My mother is a little . . . forgetful sometimes. And let us sit down."

She did so, and Mr. Brinmore followed at once, leaning forward in his eagerness to justify his presence. "It all began with my cousin Elisabeth," he said. "She's great friends with the Fermors, in the country."

It took Marianne a moment to place the name. "Oh, yes, Sir Thomas' sister."

"Right." He looked relieved. "So when I thought of coming up to town, they determined to write to Sir Thomas and his new wife." Brinmore paused, uncertain how Marianne would take this reference to her mother's remarriage, but she nodded encouragingly. "We knew no one else, you see, and I didn't like to come without any acquaintance."

"Of course not."

Brinmore looked further relieved. "Well, Lady Bentham replied that they, er, you, would be happy to make introductions. Indeed, she invited me to stay here." He looked slightly reproachful. "I have the letter in my bag."

"And when you arrived, no one seemed to know anything about it. How dreadful for you." Marianne shook her head sympathetically, but her vivid blue eyes were dancing.

"Well, it was," the young man agreed. Had anyone told him that Marianne was actually some months his junior, he would have scoffed. "If Lady Bentham has changed her mind, I can—"

"No, no. Mama simply forgot to mention it, I'm sure. I will have the servants prepare a room. It won't take a moment." Privately, Marianne gave thanks for this addition to their household. Now, at least, she would have someone of her own age to talk with.

Brinmore rose as she did, uneasy. "I don't wish to put you to any trouble. Are you sure that—"

"Nonsense! I'll just tell Hobbs."

She went out, and he sank slowly onto the sofa again. This arrival was far different from the one he had imagined. He had seen himself sweeping into an elegant London town house with perfect aplomb, and greeted with gratifying deference roused by this assurance beyond his years. In reality, he had felt like a clumsy schoolboy. Indeed, Lady Marianne reminded him strongly of his cousin Elisabeth, several years his senior and very much in charge of their household. It was almost too much.

"There," said Marianne bracingly, coming back into the room and startling him out of his reverie. "All settled. Now we can get better acquainted. Do you know you have not even told me your full name?"

Feeling an unaccountable trepidation, he said, "It's Tony. Anthony Brinmore, that is."

Strangely enough, a very similar scene was in progress less than a mile away, in the town house of Lady Sybil Goring, where Susan Wyndham was confronting an open-faced young man with brown hair and blue eyes. Her approach, however, was more direct. "Well, I do not see why you have come. It was quite unnecessary."

He smiled, the shifting planes of his face suggesting a sunny temperament combined with familiarity with Susan's habits and a certain ability to deal with them. "Mama thought it a good idea, when she heard Grandmama was ill." His smile became a grin. "She thought Cousin Georgina might want some help."

"Nonsense!"

"We'll see what Georgina says." He continued to gaze at Susan with quizzical amusement, and after a valiant attempt at offended dignity, she finally let an answering smile show. In another moment, the two were laughing together.

"Well, but, William, it is too unfair," protested Susan after a while. "I have been a model of propriety since I arrived in town. That is, except for . . ." She paused, biting her lower lip.

"Just so," replied William. "I expect Mama thought

you would benefit from the guidance of the head of the family."

"You?" She was torn between further laughter and outrage. "You are only three years older than me."

"Older than *I*," he corrected solemnly, though his blue eyes twinkled.

"Anyway," continued Susan, ignoring this, "Christopher is the head of our family."

"Not of the Wyndhams. As Mama's husband, of couse he has our respect. But I hold the title and the estate." As he said this, his joking tone disappeared, and there was something impressive about the declaration despite his youth. It was obvious that this young man took his responsibilities very seriously, and was eminently capable of fulfilling them.

But his younger sister was not affected. "Sir William Wyndham," she mocked. "I wonder you don't have a long gray beard by this time. I shall write to Mama at once and tell her there is no need to take you away from your precious estate. We are getting along splendidly."

William shifted from one foot to the other. "I . . . wish you wouldn't, Susan."

"I won't be watched over like a prisoner!"

"Who said any such thing?" He paused, seeming a little embarrassed. "The thing is, I've a fancy to see something of London. I am of age now, and . . ."

Susan's green eyes glowed. "The country squire is giving in at last," she crowed. "I thought you hated the very idea of town. I thought you did not care if you ever attended an assembly at Almack's or saw the king."

"There *are* other amusements in London," he answered loftily.

"Oh, I see. Then you will not be accompanying us to any of the *ton* parties?"

"Dash it, Susan," he began, for clearly this was not his intention.

But she dissolved in laughter and ran forward to hug him. "I am only bamming you. It will be splendid to have you here if you are not to be an odious watchdog. We will have such fun! It is too bad Nick is still at Oxford."

Her brother laughed again. "He is far happier there than in town. You know how he hates society."

"*You* changed your mind," she pointed out.

"I always liked our country entertainments," he countered. "Nick would far rather read a book."

For a moment they marveled silently at this aberration; then Susan shook her head and looked up. "Come and see all the invitations we have received just in the last week. I'm sure you can come with us to all the parties." She looked him over. "After you buy a new coat, of course."

"What's wrong with my coat?"

"Oh, William," she said in pitying accents, and turned toward the hall. Instantly he caught up to her and tweaked at the ribbon threaded through her red curls. Unfastened, they tumbled down about her shoulders. Susan whirled to snatch the ribbon back. "You beast! It took me nearly an hour to tie it up."

"Perhaps *you* should get a new coif," he retorted.

Susan lunged as if to pull his cravat. William jumped back, but in doing so his heel caught on something, and he fell heavily to the carpet. His exclamation of surprise was nearly drowned out by a yowl, and both young people turned to watch a mass of ginger fur streak for the doorway.

"Susan, you haven't brought that damned cat to London?" exclaimed Sir William.

She merely smiled. He pushed himself up and stood, looking disgusted. "You'd think that creature would improve with age. He must be . . . what, nearly fourteen?" He shook his head incredulously. "But he's as mean-tempered as ever."

"Daisy is never mean to *me*."

"And why you insist on calling him Daisy—it's ridiculous."

Susan, who had acquired the cat at an early age, shrugged. "He's used to it."

"Well, we're none of us used to *him*," muttered her brother, examining his sleeve to make sure it wasn't torn.

"Come and see the invitations," she laughed, taking his arm and urging him forward. After a moment, he yielded, and they walked out together.

Marianne MacClain's conversation was also just ending. The butler had come to say the young gentleman's room was ready, and Tony Brinmore had risen to follow him upstairs. But he paused in the drawing-room doorway, seeming uneasy. "There's one other thing," he said.

Marianne looked politely interested.

"I've, er . . ." He stopped, flushing.

Marianne wondered what could be the matter now. Her talk with their visitor had been halting. He was very like some of the young men she met at parties, awkward and tongue-tied in her presence. She found it rather wearisome. Tony seemed a pleasant-enough boy, but her visions of a replacement for her brother and his wife had dissolved.

"Actually, I've brought a dog," he blurted out.

"A dog?" she repeated, startled.

"Yes. I put him in the stables. He's so old now, you see, that I couldn't bear to leave him behind. He would have fretted so, perhaps died. I've had him for years and years."

This made their guest seem younger than ever. Marianne smiled. "That's all right. He can stay in the stables."

Tony's face cleared. His relief was almost ludicrous. "Thanks."

"Not at all. I like dogs. You must show him to me later."

His anxiety returned. "Oh, well, he's not a purebred, you know. I daresay you may find him . . . that is, he may not be your sort of dog."

Marianne could not help but laugh. "We shall see, shan't we? Now, go and settle into your room. Mama will be home for dinner, and you can meet her and Sir Thomas then."

This did not seem to lighten Tony's mood, but he nodded and turned to follow the long-suffering Hobbs.

3

The Countess of Cheane was that evening presenting an eminent Italian singer to society at a musicale, and the *haut ton* was nearly unanimous in attendance. Though genuine love of music was by no means so widespread, the event had acquired immense cachet during weeks of gossip fostered by the countess and her friends. Thus, both Marianne and Susan were able to assure the newcomers to their households that the evening was the height of fashion, and the young men accompanied them with far more enthusiasm than either would normally have shown for such an outing.

"Here we are," said Susan unnecessarily as they pulled up before the countess's house. "Those are linkboys, William. They light the way for the chairs."

"If you lean so far out, you will fall in the street," responded her brother shortly, not overpleased to be lectured on the ways of the town. Susan grimaced at him.

They went inside, and the ladies left their wraps. As they climbed the stairs to the drawing room, William hung back a little. "Do you think my coat is all right?" he asked Georgina quietly. "Susan seemed to find it hopelessly countrified."

"It is not the latest fashion," agreed Georgina,

knowing that he would see this for himself soon enough and that false reassurance would be useless. "But it is well made and you look the gentleman."

He nodded. "That should be good enough for anyone."

"There is that girl," hissed Susan over her shoulder.

"What girl?" answered Georgina in a normal voice.

"Shh! The one at the ball."

There could be no mistaking this reference, and Georgina looked up to find Marianne MacClain greeting their hostess on the landing.

"That one?" asked William admiringly. "Are you acquainted with her?"

"Shh!" repeated Susan. "Let us wait here until . . ." But more guests came up behind them, forcing their group to move up the stairs and reach the countess before Marianne's party had left her. Indeed, the press was so great that the two families were forced to walk into the drawing room together.

Susan and Marianne exchanged nods, and might have left it at that had it not been for William. Clearly struck with Marianne's charms, he requested an introduction, and this led to reciprocal presentations of Lady Bentham and her husband, Georgina, and Tony Brinmore. Lady Bentham, unconscious of any awkwardness, immediately suggested they find chairs and to Marianne's amused consternation and Susan's obvious outrage, they all sat down together near the rear of the room.

Lady Bentham was quite content to talk to her husband, and Georgina offered an occasional remark in counterpoint to their duet. William had taken care to place himself beside Marianne, leaving Susan and Tony to occupy the end of the row of gilt chairs.

"I understand this is to be a famous evening," William ventured as soon as they were settled.

"Yes, indeed," replied Marianne with a smile. "You are fond of music?"

"I? Well, tolerably fond."

"That's good. They say Signora Veldini can go on for hours, once she begins. She is to do the aria from *The Marriage of Figaro*, you know."

"Is she, by Jove? How, er, splendid." William smiled unconvincingly.

Marianne began to laugh. "I don't believe you like opera at all." As William began to protest, she added, "It doesn't matter. I don't myself. Indeed, half the people in this room will be dreadfully bored by the singing. More than half."

"But why do they come, then?"

"Why did you come?"

"Susan told me it was all the crack." He glanced at his sister accusingly, at the same time savoring the sensation of using a bit of fashionable slang he had picked up only in the last half-hour.

"Oh, it is. Undoubtedly. And that is the answer to your question. Nearly everyone is here so that they may say they *were*. A great many of the *ton* parties are like that."

"A dead bore?" wondered William, half-suspicious that she was mocking him.

Marianne nodded, her blue eyes dancing.

His suspicion confirmed, William sat straighter, his face losing some of its eager openness. He looked suddenly older, and much more dignified. "I don't see why *you* bother to attend in that case," he replied.

Marianne opened her eyes very wide. "I didn't say *I* was bored," she retorted teasingly.

"Very true." William withdrew still more, his expression freezing and his eyes, which had been so ingenuous, hardening.

Marianne's smile faded, and her russet eyebrows drew together in puzzlement. She had been playing the conventional game of flirtation. Why was he responding so coldly? It was almost as if he were offended. Too, she realized that her initial judgment of him had been incomplete. She had thought him a typical country squire, awed by town trappings and fairly uninteresting to one who had already spent a season among the *haut ton*.

There was more to his character, she saw now. He had a sternness and an air of maturity that belied callowness. "I was only joking, you know," she was moved to say.

"Obviously," was the only reply.

Marianne's frown deepened. Really, he was prickly. But some spark of interest in him made her add, "As I would with anyone. It is a way they have of talking here."

He thawed slightly. " 'They'?"

"Well, Londoners, the *ton*. I hardly count myself one of them."

"No?"

She was rather annoyed now, by his oversensitivity and the superior tone he took. But this very annoyance was intriguing. Marianne had met a variety of gentlemen since she came to town, from eager boys to blasé Corinthians, and this one was unlike any other. He seemed ready to enjoy the Season's amusements, but not to lose himself in them—neither bored nor dazzled. In an odd way, he reminded Marianne of her brother Ian. Yet that was ridiculous, she thought at once; the two were nothing alike.

"No," she found herself saying, "I come from Scotland."

"Really, Scotland? I have always wanted to try the fishing there." William smiled—not sheepishly, but to show that he was more than willing to converse rationally on almost any subject she should suggest.

"It is good, I understand," answered Marianne, smiling back. She was, she found, relieved at the change in his mood. The two of them settled happily to discuss the north, each gaining a more favorable impression of the other with every moment.

It was far otherwise with the couple on their right. Susan's first words upon sitting down were, "What a stupid place. We are much too far back. Why did not Georgina speak?"

Understandably, Tony Brinmore had no ready reply to this. He contented himself with a murmur that might be construed as assent and crossed one leg over the other in an effort to appear at ease. At first glance, Susan's elfin prettiness had attracted him, but it appeared that London girls were all intimidating, in one way or another.

Susan fumed silently for a few moments, but when her attempts to catch Georgina's eye failed, and she saw that William was not to be dislodged, she sighed audibly and turned back to the only available companion. The appraising look she gave Tony then caused him to shift uneasily in his chair. "Who are you, exactly?" she asked him.

"I . . . I beg your pardon?"

"I don't understand who you are," she repeated patiently. "You are a connection of Lady Bentham's family?"

"No. Friend of Sir Thomas' sister. That is, my

cousin is." Feeling this to be confusing, he added, "Name's Tony, Tony Brinmore."

"I heard your name," answered Susan. "So you are staying with Sir Thomas and Lady Bentham for the Season?"

He nodded warily.

"This is your first visit to London?" Susan was slightly impatient, but she was also enjoying the sense that she was more at ease than he. Since entering society, she had suffered certain shocks to her self-esteem in this area.

"Yes."

"Mine also. This sort of thing is amusing, is it not?" She waved a hand to indicate their surroundings, thrilled by the world-weary tone she had managed.

This was too much. "Have you been to a musical evening before?" inquired Tony aggressively.

"Well, I . . ."

"I suppose you know all about this"—he consulted the program sheet he had been given—"Signora Veldini? What's she like?"

"I have not actually . . ."

"No, I don't suppose you have. In fact, you know nothing whatsoever about it." He stopped abruptly and flushed at his own rudeness, then told himself that she had deserved it.

Susan Wyndham's green eyes were sparkling alarmingly. "I know more than you," she snapped. "I know, for example, that that neckcloth is wretchedly tied. It looks as if you had crumpled it in your fist."

Tony drew himself up with a gasp, his flush deepening. She had hit a sore point; he had had serious doubts about the neckcloth himself. But these were, of course, forgotten now. "I'll have you know this is a perfect Mathematical," he sputtered, using a term hastily recalled from a gentleman's periodical.

"Mathematical?" Susan sneered. "Don't be ridiculous."

Tony longed to hit her, but he also knew that he was on weak ground. He would go out and order a whole new wardrobe first thing tomorrow, he vowed. "Obviously you know nothing about fashion either," he replied loftily.

Susan began a scorching setdown, but at that moment she caught sight of Baron Ellerton making his way along the back of the room to a chair three rows behind. Immediately, Tony Brinmore was forgotten. She followed the elegant figure of the older man, and eyed with rancorous curiosity the stunning brunette by whose side he settled himself.

Tony, conscious that he had lost her attention, followed her gaze. The sight of Baron Ellerton turned his anger to glum envy. Here, clearly, was a true man of fashion, and the contrast between his appearance and Tony's own filled him with despair. It was no wonder girls laughed at him, he thought. He had to find a tailor at once. Sir Thomas would know someone.

To Tony's relief, the countess mounted the low platform that had been erected across the end of the drawing room and called her guests to order for the beginning of the program. Susan was forced to turn back, and William and Marianne to drop what had by now become an animated exchange. Slowly the hum of conversation died, and the audience fell into an anticipatory silence.

Signora Veldini's voice was impressive; it filled the room with ease. Indeed, some of the countess's guests thought it overfilled, though few would have admitted it. Too, the statuesque Italian seemed tireless. Each mark of appreciation as she finished a selection spurred her to further efforts, and the audience's enthusiasm was clearly strained by the time their hostess again mounted the platform and announced the interval. The signora looked both surprised and displeased, but the listeners rose at once, giving her no chance to protest that she was not yet at all tired.

"Who is this Figaro, anyway?" asked William as their party moved slowly toward the refreshment room. "His marriage must have been a rum go."

Marianne laughed aloud, but when William frowned, she answered, "It must indeed."

"*I* think this party is rum," put in Tony Brinmore, who had overheard. "If this is the *haut ton*'s idea of amusement, I'm sorry I ever came to London."

William turned to agree, and the two young men sized one another up approvingly, having been too occupied to do so before now. They were similar in age and height, though they did not much resemble each other. Tony's hair was dark blond to William's brown, and his eyes a sparkling hazel while William's were blue. Too, Tony's frame was rangy rather than compact. But they were drawn together by the like state of their clothes. Surrounded by male elegance, and conscious of amused glances from more than one pink of the *ton*, they warmed at once to one another. William's concern was far less than Tony's, but he saw the other's discomfort with understanding. And their total agreement about the music further cemented the bond. Before the group reached the refreshment room, the young men had made a date to visit a tailor the following day, and were talking as if they had known one another for years.

This left Marianne to chat with Georgina, for Susan was paying attention to nobody, her eyes fixed on the other guests.

"Did you enjoy the program?" Marianne inquired.

"Her voice is splendid," answered Georgina, "but I thought the selections poorly organized, and of course, she went on too long."

"You are a connoisseur, I see."

"I?" Georgina looked startled. "Oh no. I am fond of music, and attend concerts whenever I can, but my tastes are uneducated."

"Indeed, anyone can see that," teased Marianne gently. "That is why you brought your music to follow along." She indicated the morocco folder tucked under the other's arm.

Georgina flushed a little. "I had heard she was to sing the aria, and I just thought . . ."

"You needn't act as if I had caught you at something shameful. I admire your application. Do you sing?"

Seeing that she meant it, Georgina smiled. "I am a mere amateur."

"Oh yes, we have established that." The younger girl smiled again. She found Miss Goring's modesty endearing. "I wish I liked music more. My brother says I play the pianoforte as if I had no fingers, only fists. I began late in life, of course."

"You have other talents," offered Georgina.

"Do I? Perhaps." She smiled ruefully.

They reached the back parlor, where the buffet was spread, and the ladies sat round a table while the gentlemen went off to fill plates. Separated from her husband, Lady Bentham seemed to recall her social obligations, and she addressed some remark to each of them in turn, and introduced Georgina and Susan to several passing fashionables. She was just about to present another when Susan abruptly stood and moved a few steps away from the table. Startled, the others merely watched as she tossed her red curls and smiled brilliantly at an approaching gentleman—Baron Ellerton.

Whether he would have paused to speak to them was unclear, and irrelevant now, for he had no choice. He strolled back to their table beside Susan and greeted the other ladies with a pleasant smile. They had begun to exchange the usual comments about the performance when Susan blurted out, "Do sit down and join us."

Georgina could not restrain a grimace. Lady Bentham looked vaguely surprised, and Marianne's expression was a mixture of amusement, annoyance, and commiseration. The baron, unfailingly polite, agreed. "For a moment, perhaps." But he did not take the chair next to Susan, moving rather to that between Georgina and Lady Bentham.

Susan frowned, but the return of the other gentlemen with loaded plates put an end to conversation. As they were handing round their booty and finding chairs themselves, Georgina murmured, "I do beg your pardon."

Her voice was so low the baron barely heard, but he turned toward her, and Georgina's cheeks reddened a little as she repeated the apology.

"No need," he replied, smiling in a way that made Georgina's pulse quicken. He really was extraordinarily handsome, she told herself, trying to explain her uncharacteristic susceptibility. And, of course, one could not help thinking of his great position. But she had encountered men with both these attributes before during her stays in London. What was it about this one, she wondered, that affected her so acutely?

It must be embarrassment over Susan's behavior. She had never before been in charge of another when going into society.

"Why be so very concerned about Miss Susan Wyndham's, er, enthusiasms?" he asked, still smiling.

"I must be. I am in charge of her, you see, and—"

"You?"

He needn't be quite so surprised, Georgina thought, nettled. "I am well able to look after her." But even as she said it, she wished she had held her tongue. She had not demonstrated any such skill tonight or at the ball where Susan had behaved so abominably. Indeed, Georgina thought miserably, *he* had saved that situation while she stood by like a stone. She waited for a mocking setdown, which she undoubtedly deserved.

"I meant only that you are very young to be in sole charge of a comeout," he added. "And one which will most likely be, er, very lively." He smiled again, inviting her to share his mild joke and appreciating the play of expression across her face. This woman was unusual, he thought, intrigued. On the one hand, she possessed a quiet elegance of dress and demeanor that suggested aloof disinterest. Had he not spoken to her, he would have merely admired the classically severe lines of her cream silk gown and her way of holding herself, and moved on. But in conversation she revealed a susceptibility and endearing hint of uncertainty that was at odds with her cool beauty. She was, Ellerton thought, neither one thing nor the other, and he found the combination arresting.

Georgina gazed at him. He really was not mocking her, she saw with astonishment. Nor was he exhibiting the boredom and impatience she had expected to see in a very few minutes after he sat down. The expression in his eyes was interested and . . . She groped for a word. Measuring.

Georgina had not found kindness characteristic of London society. Indeed, her experience was just the opposite. In her own first Season, she had been subject to enough sly raillery and careless setdowns to last her a lifetime; and though she had changed utterly since then, her expectations had not.

Had she considered the matter beforehand, Georgina would have been certain Baron Ellerton was a supercilious, arrogant man, like many others she had encountered, and that he would have no interest whatsoever in her or her situation. Now, faced with his actual behavior, she was nonplussed.

"I feel somehow as if I have made a blunder," he said in response to her silence. "But I admit I am not certain what it is. I was not, you know, impugning either your ability or Miss Wyndham's character."

"No, no. You were . . ." Georgina faltered, wishing desperately for some of the social address he possessed in such abundance.

"Commenting on things which are none of my affair?" he finished, smiling once again. "My friends claim it is one of my most distressing failings. They find my fascination with the human comedy incomprehensible."

Some of Georgina's awkwardness dissolved in curiosity. "The human comedy?"

He gestured at the people around them. "What else can one call it? Look at Rollin Enderby, for example." He nodded toward a gentleman two tables off.

"You mean the man with the nagging wife?"

He looked astonished. "You know him?"

Georgina cursed her wayward tongue. "No, but I

. . ." She swallowed nervously. "You can see from the way he sits, and the way she is speaking to him."

Ellerton glanced at the Enderbys again, and then at Georgina, an intent expression in his vivid blue eyes. This woman impressed him more at every turn. "You can indeed. Is this your first visit to London, Miss Goring?"

She blinked. "No, I spent a Season in town some years ago. And I occasionally visit my aunt—Lady Goring."

"Ah. But we have not met."

"No."

"I wonder why?"

Georgina wondered why he should ask.

"But that is unimportant; we have met now," he went on before she could reply. "What do you think of Signora Veldini?"

Without thinking, Georgina repeated what she had said to Lady Marianne. Ellerton nodded appreciatively. "Indeed, discernment is as important to art as innate talent, is it not? Her voice is splendid, but she has no sense of pace or selection. I wonder at her great reputation."

Georgina nodded, amazed. He had clearly given thought to the subject, and his conclusions were very similar to her own. Again, he was behaving quite unlike her idea of a man of fashion.

Ellerton had by this time noticed the morocco folder, which Georgina had put under her chair. "May I?" he asked, bending to retrieve it. Before she could reply, he was flipping through the pages of music. His chestnut eyebrows rose. "Your score is in Italian."

Georgina flushed again. She had been called a bluestocking often enough, and in such insulting tones that she braced herself for an onslaught. And she found to her astonishment that she particularly dreaded such a remark from him. Moreover, it was monstrously unfair. Her studies were limited to music, for which her passion had grown as she matured.

"My compliments," he added with another smile.

Georgina searched his face for mockery, and did not find it. She could not believe he was not laughing at her. "I do not speak it," she responded hurriedly. "And I read it poorly—just for the music."

"You must be very fond of music, then." He was examining her face with interest. The more one conversed with her, he thought, the more one realized her beauty. She was not the sort of woman who could pose, statuelike, and be beautiful. Her appeal was more subtle and elusive, and closely tied to her personality.

"Yes," answered Georgina quietly. Her heart was beating very fast—because she had expected a setdown, she told herself.

"You must educate me, sometime," Ellerton went on. "I prefer to understand as well as appreciate. In all things."

Georgina glanced up, surprised again, and the look she met in his eyes froze her tongue.

At this moment, Susan, irritated beyond measure by Ellerton's lack of attention to her, leaned forward and said, "It is nearly time to go back to our seats. Will you join us, Baron Ellerton?"

Her effrontery left the others speechless. But Ellerton merely smiled slightly and rose. "I beg your pardon, but I am promised to friends." And with a nod, he took his leave.

Susan opened her mouth to protest, and Georgina plunged in, leaning forward over her plate. "Do you like the lobster patties, Susan? Have you had them before? Oh, you are eating meringues, I see. They are delicious, are they not? We must ask the countess where she purchased them. Or perhaps she has a splendid cook. I do hope not, for I should so like to get some of these."

By this time, Baron Ellerton was well way, and the other members of Georgina's group were gazing at her in mild astonishment. None of them had ever heard her utter such a string of nonsense.

The moment of danger past, Georgina subsided, and talk again became general. But Susan ignored Tony Brinmore's feeble efforts at conversation and glared balefully first at Georgina, then at the retreating figure of the baron. "He hardly spoke to *me*," she said aloud, making Georgina wince. "And after I specifically *asked* him to join us." She paused. Georgina was relieved to see that only Marianne appeared to be listening. Susan's pretty face set. "The next time, he will notice me," she assured herself with a small nod. "He will indeed."

Grorgina pushed her plate away, hunger quelled. Marianne bit her full lower lip thoughtfully for a moment, then slowly smiled. The curve of her lips, Georgina saw with a sinking heart, precisely matched that of Susan's. In fact, in the brief interval before the two girls' attention was diverted, they looked more alike than Georgina would have thought possible.

4

Two mornings later, on a very fine warm day, Marianne encountered Tony Brinmore in the front hall of the Bentham house, on the point of going out. "Where are you off to?" asked Marianne, who was feeling bored.

"Oh, engagement with William Wyndham," he answered, hand on the doorknob.

This made him even more interesting. "To go where?"

"Nowhere you'd like." Tony opened the door, his impatience to be gone obvious.

But if he had thought to discourage Marianne by these methods, he was sadly mistaken. His resistance merely increased her curiosity. "Where?" she insisted.

Tony sighed heavily. "Wyndham heard of a balloon ascension on Hampstead Heath. We're riding out to watch. It ain't the least fashionable. You wouldn't care for it."

"On the contrary, I should like it above all things. I shall come with you."

Tony's dismay was so clear that she had to laugh. "Come now, it is not so bad as that. I assure you I shall enjoy myself. I attended a balloon ascension last Season, and it was wonderful. And I shan't get in your way."

This, thought Tony, was impossible. Having charge of a female would change the whole character of the expedition. And of all females, Marianne was perhaps the last he would choose. Inspiration struck him. "You can't go alone. It's just to be Wyndham and me, you know."

"I could take my maid. But I really don't think it is necessary. You are an old friend of the family—or Sir Thomas' family, at any rate." This was weak, and Marianne hurried to divert him. "You do not mean you will refuse to let me come? You could not be so mean!"

Tony groped for a response. That was exactly what he meant, but it did seem harsh and unfeeling when she gazed at him in that reproachful way, as if he were behaving callously as well as rudely. "It ain't an expedition for girls," he responded desperately. "I'm taking Growser, and we're riding, and—"

"I can ride better than you, I wager," retorted Marianne, beginning to be angry. Why should he deny her this outing when she had been feeling so bored? she thought.

Tony felt trapped, but he did not see any way out, or any that did not include being inexcusably impolite to the daughter of his hosts. "Oh, very well," he said grudgingly.

"I'll go up and change," replied Marianne with a broad smile. "I won't be a moment."

"Mind you aren't. Wyndham will be waiting. I'll be in the stables."

When Marianne met him there some twenty minutes later, Tony was holding the reins of both their horses and looking mulish. "If that's what you call a moment—" he began.

"Oh, don't be prickly. I'm here now. Shall we go?"

Marianne started to mount, then paused as she noticed a strange dog waiting on the other side of Tony's horse. "What is that?"

Tony bristled. "That is Growser, and he is coming with us." His tone conveyed a great deal, and Marianne remembered now what he had said when he first arrived. She walked around to look at the animal. Growser was clearly of no particular breed. He was large and shaggy, brown, and, Marianne could see, very old. The hairs of his muzzle were white, and he moved with the economy of age. As she came closer, the dog looked to Tony for a sign, and receiving no demur, began to wag his short tail. His eyes, though nearly obscured by fur, were bright and good-natured.

She laughed and sank to her knees, rubbing Growser vigorously behind the ears. He wriggled in ecstasy and licked her face. Marianne laughed again.

Tony gaped, astonished that the formidable Lady Marianne would deign to notice Growser. But there could be no doubt her interest was genuine. Watching them, he smiled slightly and thawed a bit toward her.

"Will he be all right running beside the horses?" she asked, standing again.

"Oh yes. He's still lively, though he is old."

"You said you have had him a long time, I remember."

"Nearly all my life." Tony braced himself for a joke. He had often been teased about his attachment to such an unprepossessing animal.

But Marianne replied only, "We had a great many dogs when I was a child. My brother and I each had a puppy when I was small. My Sandy died three years ago, or I should have brought her to London."

Tony relented further. Perhaps, he thought, his

judgment of Marianne had been prematurely harsh. However, he said only, "We should go."

She mounted at once, and they set off for the Goring house. It was not far, and they arrived to find William waiting for them in front. Tony started to apologize for their tardiness, but before he could speak, William said, "I'm sorry, Tony, but Susan found out where I was going, and she insists upon coming along. I couldn't persuade her that she wouldn't like it, though I swear I tried my best."

Tony laughed and shook his head. "It seems we're in the same case, then." He indicated Marianne with a gesture.

William, who had been too full of his own concern to notice her until then, flushed and looked uncomfortable, wishing he had not been so vehement.

Marianne laughed aloud. "You poor things! But I daresay it won't be half so bad as you think. We shan't bother you, and now that there are to be two of us, we can keep one another company." Only to herself did she admit a slight sense of relief that the proprieties would also be satisfied.

"I didn't mean . . ." stammered William. "That is, of course I am only too happy to have you come, Lady Marianne."

"You are too kind, sir," she responded teasingly.

He looked up quickly, then smiled at the ridiculousness of the thing.

"Is your sister ready?" asked Tony in resigned tones.

"Yes, I'll get her." William walked around the corner of the house toward the stableyard.

"Alas, Mr. Brinmore, the next time you must sneak out the back door in the dead of night," teased Marianne.

"I shall," he replied feelingly, but smiled a little out of his new charity with her.

The others appeared, already mounted, and Tony and Marianne moved forward to join them. Susan had clearly been informed of the other addition to their party already, and she greeted Marianne with politeness if not with joy.

"It is rather a long ride," warned Tony, with perhaps a last lingering hope that the ladies would reconsider. "We had best get started if we are not to miss the ascension."

William and Marianne turned their horses' heads obligingly, but Susan did not stir. "Is that your dog?" she asked Tony accusingly.

He looked belligerent. "It is, and he's coming!" He braced himself to squelch any objections. He had borne enough, he told himself.

"Well, then, I am bringing Daisy," Susan declared, starting to slide to the pavement.

"Susan, no!" exclaimed her brother.

Marianne and Tony exchanged a mystified look.

"If he's bringing that creature, I don't see any reason why not," she replied, starting toward the front door.

"They'll fight. He'll get lost, and we'll spend hours looking for him. He'll . . ."

"Nonsense!" declared Susan, and disappeared inside the house.

"Oh, Lord," said Tony, goaded beyond endurance.

Marianne suppressed a laugh. "Who, or perhaps I should say what, is Daisy?" she inquired.

William sighed, "Susan's cat. Daisy is to cats what Growser is to dogs, more or less."

"Indeed?" Marianne couldn't help but laugh.

He nodded, defeated. "Except that he has the foulest temper of any cat I've ever seen."

"He?" wondered Marianne delicately.

But William merely nodded again.

"By Jove, this is too much!" exploded Tony. "I plan a simple outing, with no fuss, and it turns into a deuced circus. What next, I wonder? An elephant? Growser don't like cats."

"Mr. Brinmore! How very disobliging of you," Marianne declared, once again trying not to laugh.

"It's all very well for you," he retorted savagely. "You can just sit there and laugh. But if Growser eats her rubbishing cat, *I'll* be responsible. And I can tell you I don't relish taking on Miss Wyndham. She'd cut me to ribbons."

William made an inarticulate noise compounded of agreement and amusement, and Marianne dissolved in helpless laughter.

As Tony turned to glare at her, Susan emerged carrying a large flat basket from which protruded a ginger-colored feline head. Growser, who had been sitting patiently on the cobblestones, stood alertly.

"Oh, Lord," said Tony again.

Susan glanced at him with disdain, then walked directly up to the dog and extended her burden to within an inch of his nose. Daisy lifted his forequarters above the rim of the basket, and for an eternal moment the two animals contemplated one another. The three observers braced themselves for disaster.

Amazingly, it did not come. Daisy and Growser appeared to come to some sort of unspoken understanding; then Daisy subsided into the basket and Growser sank back on his haunches.

Even Susan was astonished. She had, William

thought ruefully, expected to kick up a row. She probably would have enjoyed it.

"Upon my soul!" said Tony. "I've never seen anything like that in my life."

"Certainly not from Daisy," agreed William.

"Can it be because they are both old?" wondered Marianne, for it was obvious that Daisy was also well along in years. "Perhaps they are too experienced to . . ."

"Growser half-killed my sister's cat not a month since," put in Tony.

"Well, whatever it is, it's deuced lucky for us," concluded William, and the other two nodded.

"William," said Susan, "are you going to help me mount, or not?"

They rode through the streets at a good pace, for they were now considerably behind the time Tony had set, and he urged them on with threats that they would miss everything. Growser, though he seemed suspicious of many of the denizens of the London thoroughfares, seemed to have no trouble keeping pace, and Daisy observed the passing scene with cynical enjoyment from his privileged position before Susan.

They reached the edge of Hampstead Heath before noon and found the ascension well under way. The scarlet balloon lay on its side in an open meadow, and a group of men surrounded its basket with various mysterious machines. The bag was about half full, and swelling with each moment.

"Oh, I am glad we arrived early," said Marianne. "Now we can watch them fill it."

"Early!" exclaimed Tony. "We have missed some of the best parts. I meant to help them lay out the bag on the ground."

"You have done so before?"

"Many times, at home. There is a man nearby who has been experimenting with balloons since soon after I went to live there. He says someday we will fly from place to place rather than riding."

"I shan't," said Susan positively. "How does it go up? I don't understand."

"They fill the balloon with a gas," replied Tony, "and it rises like a bubble in water."

William and Marianne exchanged a glance; this seemed to them a remarkably lucid and informed explanation.

"How could anything be lighter than air?" scoffed Susan. "Air is just . . . nothing." She waved her hand about to demonstrate.

"No, it isn't," replied Tony. "It's made of . . . well, different things. I don't recall exactly."

Susan shook her head, unconvinced.

"Well, how do *you* think they get up there, then?" asked Tony, stung.

"I've never seen any such thing."

He gaped. "Are you telling me you don't *believe* balloons can fly? That is the stupidest thing I've ever—"

"Look," interrupted William, to prevent an open quarrel, "that must be the man who is to go up."

"By Jove, it's Crispin!" exclaimed Tony.

"You know him?"

"Yes. He assisted at one of the ascensions at home. I must speak to him." Tony swung down and strode off before any of the others could speak.

"He might have asked us to come along," complained Susan.

"They don't want a crowd near the balloon," answered William. "Look, there's a little hill over there. We can dismount and still see everything. Come on."

They moved to this vantage point and secured their horses among some trees behind the knoll. Growser, who had accompanied them, at once set off to explore, and as he did not seem inclined to stay out of sight for any long period of time, they left him to it.

"This is fine," pronounced William. "We can see everything quite well. We might even sit on the grass." He looked to Marianne questioningly.

She assented by doing so. The turf was dry and warmed by the morning sun, and even seated, their elevated position gave them a good view.

"We're too far off to see properly," complained Susan, still standing, Daisy's basket hooked over her arm.

"Nonsense," replied her brother. "It is much easier to tell what is going on from here. We can sort things out. Look, the balloon is beginning to rise from the ground."

They all watched as the great gas bag hesitantly lifted. Gradually, by fits and starts, it shifted from horizontal to vertical, floating above its wicker hamper.

"Oh," said Susan when it at last towered above them. She sank down beside the others and stared upward.

"Impressive," commented William.

"I am always amazed when I see a balloon," agreed Marianne. "I wonder how anyone could have thought of such a thing. There seem to be so many intricate parts, and such calculations involved." She gestured toward the lacing of guy wires and ropes, the machinery on the ground, and the red sphere now flowering above them. "I can see how one might invent any *one*, but the whole?" She shook her head, and William nodded.

"Look," said Susan, pointing. "Mr. Brinmore is helping them." Tony was indeed working with the team of men preparing for the ascent, and he appeared to know exactly what he was doing.

They watched in silence for a while. The balloon began to strain upward on its ropes, as if eager to leave the earth. Daisy, whose basket had been placed on the grass before Susan, took advantage of their preoccupation to climb out and examine his surroundings.

At last, all seemed ready. The aeronaut clambered into the car, and his helpers moved back a bit, their hands on the ropes. Only Tony remained close, chatting with the man. The three on the hill stood again in sheer excitement; the ascent seemed imminent.

Without warning, a mass of shaggy brown fur erupted from the wood behind the meadow and pelted toward Tony. Before anyone even saw to give warning, Growser had passed the circle of men and hurled himself on his master, in some mistaken effort, perhaps, to lend him aid. Tony, taken utterly by surprise, fell back under the onslaught, and Growser's momentum carried him on, right into the balloon's car. At that moment, by prearrangement, the men holding the ropes let go, and the balloon leapt upward.

They heard Tony's shout all across the meadow. His friends saw him jump wildly to catch one of the trailing lines, and fail. William rushed down to join him, but by this time the balloon was well out of reach.

"How dreadful," said Marianne. Gazing upward, her eyes shaded from the sun, she could just see Growser. The balloonist was apparently restraining the dog from leaping out of the car again. "We should have watched him more carefully."

"He should take care of his own dog," retorted Susan, and this thought leading naturally to another, she looked down. "Daisy is gone!"

Several minutes of complete disorder followed. Tony and William remained among the balloon crew, calculating the direction the vehicle was likely to take and its probable place of descent. Marianne and Susan scoured the nearby wood for the cat, Marianne growing more and more exasperated. Finally, when she heard William calling their names, she said, "He might be anywhere, even in a tree. We shall never find him. I'm going back to see what your brother means to do now."

"You can't just give up!"

"Can I not?" Marianne turned and picked her way back toward the meadow, holding up the trailing skirts of her riding habit and railing silently each time they were snagged on a branch or weed. It did nothing to improve her temper when, just at the edge of the trees, her hat caught and was pulled nearly from her head, leaving her coif in disarray.

Thus, when William greeted her by saying, "Whatever have you been doing?" she snapped, "Searching for your sister's wretched cat!" in a tone that left no doubt as to her opinion of wandering pets.

William looked puzzled, then simply pointed to the top of the knoll, where Daisy's basket still sat. In it, looking hugely self-congratulatory, sat Daisy himself. As Marianne watched, he began to clean his front paw, oozing virtue.

Marianne put her face in her hands and made an exasperated noise. Then, looking up again, she began to laugh. "Why haven't you wrung that animal's neck long since?"

"Susan," replied William, unsurprised by the question.

"Well, you must find *her* now, and I do not intend to help you." Marianne strode determinedly to the little hill, sat down beside Daisy, and fixed him with a baleful stare. "You can bring her back here."

Hiding a smile, William set off in the direction from which Marianne had come. He had scarcely left when Tony approached the knoll. "Where *is* everyone?" he asked in aggrieved tones.

Marianne did not care to discuss this. "What are you going to do? Growser will be all right, won't he?"

"As long as Crispin keeps him in the car. I'm going after him, of course."

"But how will you find him?"

"The direction and speed of the wind give one a pretty good idea where he will come down. And I shall follow the balloon." He spoke absently, most of his attention on the floating sphere, which would soon be out of sight behind the trees. "I must go. Will you tell the others, please?"

"Can we not help?"

Tony shook his head, still focused on the balloon, and went to fetch his horse. William and Susan emerged as he was mounting up.

"We shall all go," insisted Susan when his plan was repeated.

"No," said Tony flatly, and it was clear that he would brook no argument.

"I should come, at least," added William, "but . . ."

"You must escort the girls home," finished Tony. "Besides, I don't need help."

William, who obviously very much wished to go,

help or no, could not dispute this, though Marianne halfheartedly protested that they could return home on their own. In fact, she did not relish the idea at all.

Tony had turned his mount and started off when a high-pitched voice from behind them hailed Marianne. Turning, she scanned the crowd quickly, then answered, "Mrs. Gregg, how do you do?"

"Did you see the balloon? Such excitement. A dog jumped in; at least, I believe it was a dog."

Marianne nodded.

"Have you no carriage?" Mrs. Gregg seemed shocked by this. "But you cannot ride so far. Come with me. There is plenty of room."

Under any other circumstances, Marianne would not have considered it. But she saw William's eager look, quickly suppressed, and resigned herself to the drive with a woman she did not much like. As soon as she accepted, William grinned delightedly, saluted her, and rode off before Susan could object, as he was certain she would. It was left only for the girls to tie their horses to the back of Mrs. Gregg's barouche and climb in.

"Why did you say yes?" hissed Susan furiously as they did so. "We might just as well have gone with William. Or ridden home alone."

"Shh," replied Marianne. "She will hear."

"I don't care if she does."

"Well, you should. Mrs. Gregg is one of the greatest gossips in the *ton*. She knows everything that goes on, and everyone listens to her."

This gave Susan pause, and she said no more as they walked around to the door of the barouche. They took the forward seat, as Mrs. Gregg and her female companion occupied the other, and Marianne staunchly resisted the former's attempts to shift her browbeaten friend to the less comfortable position. As soon as they settled, Mrs. Gregg signaled departure. "For I am promised to the Duchess of Devonshire for tea, my dears."

They talked at first of the ascension, Mrs. Gregg speculating about the disruption and the girls not letting on that they knew any of the participants. This subject exhausted, their hostess turned to contemplate her passengers. "You are two very famous young ladies now, you know," she said, her tone teasing but not benevolent. "Your trick of wearing the same dress to the Millshires' ball is causing all sorts of talk."

Marianne felt Susan stiffen beside her, and wished they had ridden home unescorted after all. "It was a good joke, wasn't it?" she said lightly.

Mrs. Gregg tittered. "Prodigious good. But you know the strangest thing? Though the story is that you are dearest friends, I swear I never heard Lady Marianne mention Miss Wyndham before now."

"Susan was in the country," answered Marianne as if suprised. "There was no occasion to mention her. I know how tedious it is to be always talking of absent friends with whom one's listeners are wholly unacquainted."

"Very true," acknowledged Mrs. Gregg, who often did so. "Still, it seems queer." She looked from one to the other of the girls. "Wyndham. Now, that name is familiar. Where can I have heard it?" She made a great show of pondering this question. "I have it! Sybil Goring's daughter married a Wyndham. And was she not in town for the Season several years ago? Yes, that's it." She allowed a look of surprise to cross her sharp features. "Oh, my, yes. Well! You do have a great deal in common, do you not?"

"What do you mean?" asked Susan, sensing some slight to her mother.

Mrs. Gregg raised her thin eyebrows. "You *are* Anabel Wyndham's daughter?"

"Yes." Susan was truculent. Marianne tried to catch her eye, and failed.

"Well, Anabel jilted Norbury, you know. One of the most brilliant matches in England. It was a nine days' wonder. And then, of course, Lady Marianne did the same last season." She tittered again. "Not Norbury, poor man. He is long since married and, they say, sadly afflicted by the gout. But Devere. It comes to the same thing. Amazing." She paused, gauging the effect of her words on them. "And then both your mothers have married a second time. I always say that more than one marriage is, well, a bit excessive."

"It is certainly more than most can manage," replied Marianne dryly. Mrs. Gregg, who was said to have tyrannized over her late husband in the most shocking manner, was notorious for her relentless pursuit of another.

"The indulgence of calf love is so rare past a certain age," retorted the older woman. "And a trifle odd, don't you think?"

This time Marianne stiffened, at this clear hit at her mother. Both girls were by this time thoroughly incensed, a condition which drew them together.

Mrs. Gregg, seeing it, smiled a predatory smile. This was her invariable method. She had found that making people furiously angry often elicited the most interesting tidbits. They said things in the heat of rage that they would not have dreamed of uttering with a cool head. And it was obvious that Susan Wyndham, at least, was prime material.

Marianne realized it also, and with a supreme effort, she controlled her anger. There could be no satisfaction in lashing out at Lavinia Gregg. One's heated remarks would only be retailed to the *ton* and made mock of. But how, she wondered, was she to convey this to Susan, who was clearly choking with rage. She racked her brain, but could think of nothing. Then, providentially, she happened to glance down. Daisy's basket had been placed on the floor of the barouche, between her feet and Susan's. It had been carefully closed, but now she nudged it with her toe. The lid moved a little.

Susan felt it, and also looked down. Marianne pushed the basket again, at the same time turning to gaze innocently out at the passing countryside. Susan looked startled for a moment, then slowly began to smile. The basket was concealed by their skirts, and neither of the others could see as she added her efforts to Marianne's.

Disappointed by their silence, Mrs. Gregg tried again. "There is something so, ah, ridiculous, about an older person mooning about in public, don't you think? Why, I—" Her voice rose to a screech as Daisy catapulted from his basket, enraged by the jostling, and snarled himself thoroughly in the ladies' mingled skirts.

"Oh, dear," exclaimed Marianne, her voice shaking with suppressed laughter. "Susan's cat has gotten loose."

Daisy snarled, and fought with tooth and claw to free himself from the mass of gown and petticoat, entangling himself still further.

"Ow, ow," squealed Mrs. Gregg. "It is biting me! Get it away!"

"Daisy, Daisy, stop it this instant," declared Susan, bending as if to free the cat, but in reality hiding paroxysms of giggles. Seeing her shaking shoulders, Marianne put a hand on her back to keep her down.

Mrs. Gregg's companion, hitherto totally silent, now began to scream at the top of her lungs, as Daisy worked his way deeper into the flounces. The coachman pulled up in consternation, and several passing riders paused and stared.

"Get it out! Get it out!" cried Mrs. Gregg again.

Marianne signaled to Susan with a pressure on her hand that this was enough. At first, it seemed that Susan would not respond, but then she bent even further and managed to imprison Daisy in her own petticoat. Making soothing sounds, she began to extricate him from its folds.

Mrs. Gregg watched with tremulous horror. "I won't have it in my carriage," she declared. "That animal is obviously mad. It should be destroyed at once."

"I am so sorry, Mrs. Gregg," replied Marianne sweetly. "But he was only frightened, you know, at being caught. Susan will put him back in his basket."

"I won't have it in the carriage," she insisted.

"Oh?" Marianne looked around. "Well, we are nearly home. We will ride from here then."

Even in her outrage, Mrs. Gregg saw that this was going rather far. "I do not wish to force *you* out," she said.

"I quite understand. Come, Susan."

The girls climbed down, leaving their erstwhile interrogator feeling vaguely bested, and mounted from the barouche step. Bowing to Mrs. Gregg and her friend, and brushing aside another protest, they set off at a brisk trot.

"That was wonderful!" exclaimed Susan when they were out of earshot. "I thought I should die laughing."

"Let us hope that when she tells the story we do not come off too badly," answered Marianne.

"I don't care a fig what she says."

"You should. You saw what a wicked tongue she has."

"The spiteful creature. I wish Daisy had truly bitten her—hard!"

"I expect he did. He bit *me*."

"And me." Susan giggled. "But it didn't really hurt. It was a *splendid* idea. I should have said something really dreadful in another minute."

"I know."

Susan turned to look at her. "You are not so bad after all."

"I beg your pardon?"

"When we first met, I thought I should hate you."

"My dear Miss Wyndham!"

"Well, you seemed so odiously superior. And there was the dress."

"Yes, there was that," responded Marianne dryly.

"But you are not stuffy and arrogant, really."

"Thank you very much."

"Indeed, I think we are rather alike." She meant this as a compliment, but it filled Marianne with dismay. "Mind, this does not mean that I shall give in over the baron."

"Give in? What do you mean?"

"We are still rivals there."

"Rivals?" Marianne was lost.

"Oh, don't pretend you don't understand me. But I shall fight fair."

"My dear Miss Wyndham—" began Marianne again.

But Susan was diverted. "There is our street. Come on, Georgina will be very cross with me for going out without telling her where."

She kicked her horse's flanks, and Marianne was forced to follow, still protesting. Susan ignored her, sliding from her mount almost before it stopped and skipping up to the front door. In the ensuing flurry of greeting, explanation, and arrangements for a groom to escort Marianne home, the subject was lost. But Marianne found she had much to think of as she made her own way home somewhat later.

5

Tony did not return home that night, and Marianne grew rather concerned, though she reassured her mother and Sir Thomas. She rose and breakfasted early, and by eight was sitting in the drawing room writing a letter to her brother and listening for sounds of an arrival downstairs. But she found composition more difficult than usual. Never a facile letter writer, this morning she was sadly unable to concentrate on her page. She was, she realized, more worried about Tony than she would have expected. The outing yesterday had been unlike any she had had in London before. Indeed, she realized now, it had been far more like an expedition she and her brother had made as children in Scotland—a bit disorganized and haphazard, filled with misadventures, and, she was surprised to acknowledge, a great deal of fun.

Thinking of Tony and his dog, of William's criticisms of his sister's cat, and of the very unusual Miss Susan Wyndham herself, Marianne had to smile. This idea of a rivalry between them was quite ridiculous; she did not understand exactly how Susan had gotten it into her head. Baron Ellerton was unlikely to take serious notice of either of them.

Thinking of such issues brought Marianne round to the question of marriage. She had pondered it a good deal in the past year, as must any intelligent young lady involved in the London Season. The festivities were so often directed at that one thing—to marry off the younger generation of the *ton*—that it could scarcely be ignored. And Marianne's own experience in refusing one of the most eligible noblemen in England had brought the matter home to her as no abstract imagining could do.

She wished to marry; she had no doubt on that score. But she was not at all certain what sort of man she would accept. Before she had come to town, sequestered in the wilds of Scotland, she had vowed to wed a thorough Londoner, who would guarantee her a round of gaiety from the capital, to Brighton, to Leicestershire. But when such a man had actually offered, she had not hesitated to refuse, despite the furor this caused. She had simply known that they would not suit. But this had left her perplexed about her own desires. What sort of life did she really want, having now tasted the pleasures of society?

This again called up the image of Ellerton. He was, on the one hand, everything she had dreamed of as a young girl—elegant, assured, a leader of society. Yet he was more, too. Marianne could not imagine Lord Robert Devere, whose proposal she had refused, taking the trouble to aid two near-strangers in a ballroom, or good-humoredly giving in to an importunate request to join a party in which he could have little interest. These were trifling things, she admitted to herself, but trifling things could be important. Was he the sort of man she had been unconsciously searching for? Smiling slightly, Marianne concluded that there might be something in what Susan Wyndham said after all.

Oddly enough, in Lady Goring's house not too far

away, Georgina Goring was following a similar train of thought. This was odd not only because of the coincidence, but because Georgina almost never thought of marriage. Ten years ago, she had done so. Sent to town against her will, and far from successful among the *ton*, she had developed a severe case of calf love for the man Susan's mother had eventually wed. He had been very kind to the difficult girl she was then, and she would have married him in an instant—no doubt to regret it bitterly later. But there had been no question of that, and she had soon realized it, with a good deal of pain. However, this period of intense emotion had taught her a great deal about people, which her isolated childhood had not, and it had changed her from a withdrawn, overplump schoolgirl to a slender, thoughtful young lady. Indeed, she believed it had been a chief force in shaping her character, which she knew to be unusual. She looked back on it now with a queer kind of gratitude. Without that hurt, she felt, she would be far less than she was.

But it had discouraged her thoughts of marriage. She had met no other man she liked so well, and when she returned to her father's house, she found she was content there. She resisted her aunt's frequent invitations to spend further Seasons in town, and evolved her own pleasant routine at home. The death of her father had been hard, but it had not made her wish for any other life.

Yet she was not feeling as unhappy as she had expected, forced this Season to stay in town and reenter the social lists. She found that she looked forward to the ball they were to attend that evening, and to the other events that would come after it.

And one of the chief reasons for this reversal, she had to admit to herself, was Baron Ellerton.

Georgina did not see how this could be. She prided herself on her common sense, and this side of her jeered at the notion that the baron might be interested in her when he had all society to choose from. Yet some hitherto dormant part of her persisted in calling up Ellerton's handsome countenance, pointing out the warm look in his eyes when he had joked with her, and daring to hint that perhaps Georgina had simply never met the right sort of man before and that this was her time.

"Nonsense!" she said aloud to herself, determinedly picking up the sewing she had allowed to fall in her lap. "I've never heard anything so ridiculous in my life. You are falling into a premature dotage. *And* acting just as you did at eighteen, when you 'fell in love' with a man who was kind to you but had no further interest." This silenced that unfamiliar voice in her mind, and Georginia flushed at the thought that she was merely repeating her earlier mistake.

Susan Wyndham, in her bedchamber upstairs, was prey to no such doubts. Her only thought, in fact, was for the gown she would wear to the ball that night, and its probable effect on the gentleman who was occupying so many feminine brains.

The ballooning party came together again for the first time at the ball. Tony and William had reached home late in the afternoon, too late for explanations, and they had agreed between them to ride to the ball, avoiding stuffy carriages. Thus, the girls were forced to wait until the two gentlemen entered the ballroom to get any information. Fortunately, this occurred between sets, and Susan and Marianne immediately deserted the groups with whom they had been chatting and descended on the newcomers. Georgina, who had heard the full story from Susan, strolled over more slowly, interested to learn the outcome.

"You selfish beast," was the first remark she heard, addressed to Sir William by his sister. "Why did you not come and tell me everything at once? When Gibbs said you had come home and gone out again, I—"

"Do you want to hear it now?" retorted William, "or would you prefer to abuse me in front of all London?"

With a ferocious grimace, Susan subsided.

"Well, we got him back," continued William.

"Growser is all right?" asked Marianne, who had become rather attached to him in her short acquaintance.

"Oh yes." This was from Tony. "He's always getting into scrapes, and he is never hurt. I believe Crispin was worse off when we reached them. Growser would jump about, and the poor man looked quite green."

They all laughed.

"Where did you find him?" asked Marianne. "It must have been quite a distance away."

Tony nodded. "The dratted wind carried them nearly twenty miles, and Crispin was afraid to try to descend through it with Growser there. He had to wait for sunset. By the time he got down and we helped him secure the balloon, it was too late to come home. We stayed at an inn nearby."

"And slept half the morning," commented Susan acidly.

The two young men looked sheepish, and Georgina and Marianne smiled, thinking it very likely that they had celebrated the rescue of Growser by indulging rather too freely in the inn's beer. Both were a bit pale.

"We rode home pretty slowly," acknowledged William. He and Tony exchanged a conspiratorial glance. It was obvious that their budding friendship had been cemented by this shared adventure.

"Well, you missed Almack's," answered his sister. "We went last night."

"Remind me to buy Growser three pounds of steak," said William to Tony, who grinned.

Susan made an exasperated sound, but before her brother could bait her further, there was a stir at the door and Baron Ellerton strolled in, looking the picture of elegance and ease.

At once, all three women's attention shifted. Though they moved only slightly, it was clear even to Tony that their interest was elsewhere.

"Good evening, Baron," said Susan.

He nodded, smiled, and returned the greeting, including the others. Georgina and Marianne murmured acknowledgments. In the corner, the musicians began again.

"Oh, a waltz," exclaimed Susan. "Do you know, Baron Ellerton, I only last night received the sanction of Princess Lieven to waltz." She gazed up at him so meaningfully that Georgina had to repress a gasp. She might as well ask *him* to dance, she thought.

"I congratulate you," replied Ellerton, surveying the ladies with a slightly wider smile. They formed a striking picture—Susan exquisite and deceptively fragile in pale green muslin, Marianne magnificent in blue satin exactly the shade of her eyes, and Georgina delicately distinguished between the two redheads in dove satin with an overlay of spidery gray lace.

"It is such an exhilarating dance," dared Susan. This time, Georgina could not suppress her intake of breath.

Ellerton, hearing it, met her shocked gaze with dancing eyes. Georgina's mortification eased as she realized that the baron was more than up to this contest. Indeed, he was completely in charge. "Some say so," he agreed. "If you will excuse me, I must claim my partner."

With a slight bow, he turned away, walking along the side of the room to the daughter of the Duchess of Lancombe, who welcomed him with a brilliant smile.

The ladies turned back to Tony and William, Susan clearly piqued, Marianne thoughtful, and Georgina flushed with embarrassment, both for Susan's boldness and her own ridiculous hopes.

"Fellow thinks he's quite something," murmured Tony to William.

"Umm," was the only reply. William was following the baron with his eyes, taking in the cut of his coat and the chaste austerity of his waistcoat. He had been deeply affected by the ladies' behavior. That even Georgina, whom he thought of as a kind of aunt, should forget his existence when confronted by Ellerton filled him with annoyance. And Marianne's desertion piqued him so sharply that he began to reconsider his refusal to waste money on new clothes. He had discouraged Tony from replacing his wardrobe, urging him to what William thought more important outings such as visiting Manton's shooting gallery and Jackson's boxing saloon. But now he wondered if he had been mistaken. Marianne's opinion was of increasing interest to him, and he did not want to neglect any possible advantage, however trivial it might seem to him.

Tony was even more affected. He had been worried about his clothes in any case, no matter what William said, and he had quite enjoyed being the object of several pairs of enthralled feminine eyes. The abrupt severing of this attention, and the obvious reason, put him on his mettle. "Must see that snyder tomorrow first thing," he muttered.

William nodded. To add to his chagrin, an unknown young man came up at that moment and requested Marianne's hand for the waltz. William, who had intended to do this himself, glowered as they went off to join the set.

Tony looked hunted. He had no wish to partner the spitfire Miss Wyndham, but politeness dictated that he dance, and custom urged that he not leave sister and brother to each other. Swallowing to find his voice, he heroically made his request. Susan accepted with scant grace, and they too departed.

"Georgina?" said William, ruthlessly pushing back his annoyance. He liked Georgina very well, and it was by no means a penance to dance with her, though neither was it like dancing with Lady Marianne.

Georgina laughed, conscious of the trend of his thoughts. "You needn't, William. I shall go and sit with the chaperons, where I belong." She felt a pang as she said this, but she told herself fiercely that it was no more than the truth.

"Nonsense!" responded her young cousin. "You can't leave me standing here. I don't know any other young ladies, and they will all wonder what is the matter with me that you will not dance."

She laughed again. "Very well. We cannot let that

happen. But when this set is finished, I will present you to some of them."

"Agreed," responded William with an answering smile, and they turned to join the set.

The waltz gave way to a country dance, and a cotillion, and a quadrille. Tony and the Wyndhams broadened their acquaintance with the aid of Marianne and those she presented. They went in to supper with a lively group and obviously were enjoying the evening, thought Georgina, sitting on the edge of the boisterous party. She herself was less content. She didn't feel much akin to young girls just out of the schoolroom and young men years younger than she; yet when she sat down with the chaperons, she felt equally out of place. She knew none of them well, and it was always clear to her that they wished to gossip about matters they felt unsuitable for the ears of an unmarried woman, whatever her age. Whenever Georgina took a chair in their circle, the conversation died, and then began again, usually with a kindly inquiry about her family or her charge. Georgina felt distinctly in the way, and heartily sick of assuring them that Lady Goring was indeed on the mend, or that Susan was not the least trouble. The sweetly probing questions about Susan were the worst, for Georgina had the feeling that the older women shared her sense that Susan would do something outrageous before the Season ended. They, however, awaited developments with avid relish. Their only amusement, so far as Georgina could see, was scandal.

Thus, Georgina was neither one thing nor the other, and she wondered as the supper interval concluded how she would get through an entire Season hanging on the fringes of two incompatible groups.

If only Aunt Sybil would regain her health, she wished silently, she could return to her own good friends in the country. There, she did not feel alien. Indeed, she knew she was admired and respected. But Lady Goring seemed the same each day when she visited her—bright-eyed and interested in all the news, yet still very weak.

Georgina followed her cousins back into the ballroom with these thoughts uppermost in her mind. As the music began once again, and the young people paired off for the dance, she looked about for a retreat. The chaperons were still at supper, their deserted corner a jumble of gilt chairs and blue velvet sofas. She did not want to sit there. Looking further, Georgina noticed that the long windows that marched down the far side of the chamber were recessed. Behind their draperies were shallow niches hidden from the crowd.

She edged her way around the walls, nodding to several acquaintances but not stopping, until she was in front of the first embrasure. The hangings were firmly closed, their hosts not being proponents of the advantages of fresh air. Glancing quickly about to see that no one was observing her, Georgina pulled a gilt chair through the curtains and let them swing shut behind. Her heart was beating fast at this most unconventional act, and she stood very still for a long moment, awaiting discovery. But it did not come. After a while she took a deep breath and sat down, relaxing for perhaps the first time that evening.

As she recovered her composure, she leaned back in the chair, breathed deeply again, and looked about her. Her refuge was snug; the draperies brushed her left arm, and her right was almost against the cool windowpanes. She could see the back garden dimly, and the sounds of the ball were perfectly clear, though she was no longer, she felt, really a part of it. Her confidence growing, she pushed open a tiny slit in the curtains and watched the dancers whirl by. A guilty thrill ran through her. This surreptitious security was somehow very appealing. She need not worry whether people were staring and commenting on her social ineptitude, yet she could still do her duty to Susan.

Sheepishly content, Georgina watched one set give way to another, and another. The night waned, and she regretfully acknowledged that it was time to leave her hiding place and rejoin the crowd. Susan and William would be looking for her soon. She would, however, remember this shift, she assured herself; next time, she might even try to bring a novel.

The last set struck up, a waltz, and Georgina rose and prepared to emerge. But before she could do so, the curtain was pulled back slightly and Baron Ellerton leaned inside. "Will you dance?" he asked, as if there were nothing peculiar in finding a partner behind the draperies.

Georgina flushed scarlet, unable to answer for embarrassment. But the baron took her silence for assent and pulled her hand through his arm. Georgina walked onto the floor in a daze and followed his lead mechanically as he swung her into the set. Then, swallowing to ease her dry throat, she stammered, "I . . . I dropped my bracelet. I was searching for it."

Ellerton glanced at her silver-gilt ornament. "And you found it. My congratulations."

From his tone, Georgina could tell that he knew it a lie. She ventured an upward glance and saw that his blue eyes were dancing, but with mirth, not mockery. "Did you see me go in?" she asked in a small voice.

"Some time ago," he agreed, letting the smile he had been restraining appear. "I did not wish to disturb you, but as this was the last set, I suspected you would be coming out."

Georgina gazed at her feet, flushing again. "What a fool you must think me. I . . . I just wished to sit quietly for a moment."

"Or a bit longer," he suggested mischievously.

She dissolved in despair. To appear ridiculous was bad enough, but to be unmasked by this man, who seemed never to make a false step or an awkward remark, was too much. His good opinion, she realized, would have meant more than the whole *ton*'s. She wished she had never come to London.

"I beg your pardon," he added. "I shouldn't tease you. I know precisely how you feel."

She raised her eyes, embarrassment forgotten in astonishment.

Ellerton smiled again. "It that so surprising? Many must wish for a quiet retreat, at times, at these affairs. They simply haven't the courage to admit it, far less to act on the feeling." He gazed down at her with a mixture of amusement and admiration. "Indeed, I have never before met anyone who would do as you did."

Georgina was not certain this was a compliment. "You are making fun of me," she accused.

"Not at all." He paused, then added, "Well, perhaps a little. If you could have seen your furtive look as you disappeared through the curtains." His smile encouraged her to share the joke. Slowly, reluctantly, Georgina began to smile also. The picture he painted was ridiculous.

"What do you suppose the servants will think when they find your chair?" he wondered.

Georgina laughed aloud.

"That's better." He guided her through an effortless turn. Georgina was abruptly conscious of his arm firm about her waist and his hand warm in hers. He was really very close. Her shaky composure disappeared again.

He seemed to sense her withdrawal. "I imagine they will put it down to an assignation," he continued. "A lovestruck swain awaiting his inamorala. Clandestinely, of course."

This did nothing to restore Georgina's poise—quite the reverse, in fact.

"Yes," he went on, "they will concoct a torrid history, I'm certain. I can almost hear them."

So could Georgina, with a vividness that made her wish for the first time in her life for a less lively imagination. The fact that she was enfolded in a man's embrace only made it worse. Could he not see how uncomfortable this talk was making her? Venturing a look, and meeting gleaming blue eyes, Georgina indignantly concluded that he did see—exactly. Why was he doing this? Some of her uneasiness dissolved in anger. "I don't find it so easy to think like a servant," she retorted.

"Good, very good," he replied. "A distinct hit."

She gaped at him.

"One is forced to extreme measures to break through your reserve, Miss Goring."

"My . . . reserve?" She was amazed. She had never thought of herself as reserved, merely awkward.

"What do you call it? You clearly have an interesting personality, but it is very difficult to reach. That is why I asked you to dance just now. I thought that you would be more approachable, caught coming out of your hiding place."

"But you . . . why should you care?" Georgina's hopes rose again. Could the distinguished Baron Ellerton really find her engaging?

He smiled again. "It is not so often one encounters an unusual character." He indicated the dancers around them. "By and large, the *ton* is boring—the same gossip year after year, though the names change, the same round of parties and flirtations. I have become something of a connoisseur of character as a result. I am always on the lookout for a refreshing view, a new outlook. I believe you have one." He did not add that he also found her distinctively lovely. He did not want her to think he was mouthing empty compliments, as did so many of the town bucks.

So she was an object of curiosity, thought Georgina resentfully. An oddity, whose strange behavior had piqued his interest. And perhaps, though he didn't say so, he pitied her as well. He must know that she did not fit in in London. Perhaps he habitually befriended such people. She scorned his charity. "You're quite mistaken," she answered in a light tone. "I have no views whatsoever."

He looked surprised at the coldness in her voice. Obviously she had misunderstood him. Gazing at her delicately etched features, Ellerton felt, for perhaps the first time in his life, at a loss. He understood that he had gone wrong, but not precisely how. Observing and savoring the foibles of his fellow human beings was one of the chief joys of the baron's life. It did indeed, as he had said, prevent the boredom that an intelligent and thoughtful man might otherwise have felt. And he had thought that in Georgina he had found one of the rare individuals who shared his predilection, and had the necessary sharpness to practice it.

The combination of this possibility with her beauty and manner entranced him. He had not been flirting; he had been trying to share something important to him. He had thought his tone showed this, forgetting to make allowance for Georgina's far narrower experience in society.

Now he could not decide what to say to mend things. With almost any other woman, he would have known. But precisely the qualities that drew him to Georgina made it impossible for him to predict her response. She was unique in his experience and, he realized, increasingly important to him. Feeling such clumsiness as he had not since sixteen, he groped for words. He determined on honesty, partly by default. "I have offended you somehow. I beg your pardon."

Georgina looked up, startled. Her gray eyes met his vivid blue ones and held.

"Once again, I do not see exactly *how*," he added with a wry smile. "But I am very sorry. You are deucedly easy to offend."

"I am no such thing!" she protested, shocked at the accusation. Georgina thought of herself as unusually even-tempered and understanding.

"Yet I seem to repeatedly offend," he replied. "It does not happen with others."

"You are one of the *haut ton*," said Georgina, "and I come from quite another circle. Our habits are, er, very different."

"Mine being beneath contempt?"

"I didn't say . . ."

"It was obvious from your tone. So you despise me for my mode of living?"

"No!" Georgina was appalled. "It is rather you who . . ." She broke off abruptly.

He looked inquiring, and a little angry.

"London society despises all who choose to live otherwise," added Georgina carefully. "I have seen it over and over."

"And this is what you think of me?" His voice was hard.

Georgina cringed. "No. You have been . . . you do not seem . . . Oh, why can I never say what I mean?"

This last came out as a wail, and Ellerton's expression softened slightly. "We both seem to be having difficulty, Miss Goring. But may I at least assure you that I *meant* no offense?"

She met his eyes again. The sounds of conversation and music about them seemed to recede, and Georgina was again acutely conscious of his embrace. Her heart pounded. Slowly she nodded.

"Perhaps I have gone a bit too fast," he continued. "Could we start again as friends?"

"Friends?" The word seemed to echo in Georgina's ears, and she was not certain whether she felt glad or sorry. It seemed a pallid offer, yet his eyes suggested much more.

"On the way to becoming friends," he amended. "Never a bad beginning."

Hesitantly she nodded again. Ellerton smiled, and after a moment she did too. Something seemed to tremble in the balance; then, to Georgina's intense chagrin, the music ended, and she was forced to step out of his arms.

In the next instant, Susan was upon them, looking thunderous, and Georgina's only thought was to get away. She practically dragged her cousin out of earshot, and she was by no means certain the baron did not hear Susan say, "*You* danced with him!"

Their ride home was anything but pleasant as the girl deplored this development and insistently questioned Georgina about what he had said and why he had stood up with her. Georgina refused to be drawn, however, finally forcing Susan to ominous silence. But though she retained her outward composure, Georgina's thoughts were far from tranquil.

6

The following morning Tony and William went together to a tailor recommended by Sir Thomas Bentham, and by dint of Tony's insistence, and rather more money than either had thought of spending, contrived to receive their new clothing in a very few days. Thus, when a much-talked-of new play opened in the following week, the young men were able to attend decked out in their new finery. The females of their households were also present, in the first row of boxes, and had a full view of their sartorial splendor below.

"Well, I think Tony looks ridiculous," stated Susan when she had examined them both. Despite all Georgina could say, the four young people had fallen into using first names. "William looks fine, but Tony . . ." She shrugged and shook her head.

Georgina surveyed the two young men in the orchestra. Their taste had taken them in different directions. William had followed the Corinthians such as Baron Ellerton; he wore a dark blue coat and buff pantaloons with a plain waistcoat. His shirt points were moderate, and his neckcloth a fairly simple mode admirably executed. Georgina had complimented him on his appearance earlier in the evening.

Tony had been seduced by the fashion of the

dandies. His bottle-green coat was stiffened and padded into a kind of torture device, or so it seemed to Georgina. His waistcoat was a rainbow of color, adorned by a profusion of fobs. She knew he could not turn his head in his starched collar, for she had seen him rotate his whole body to look behind when William pointed out an acquaintance. Yet he looked pleased with himself, Georgina thought, and that was probably the important thing. "He is striking," she replied mildly.

Susan laughed. "One cannot miss him," she agreed derisively.

Georgina sighed softly and went back to watching the arrivals. Susan had been more difficult than ever in recent days, and she was weary enough of her carping to make no effort at conversation. Her own concerns were more than enough to occupy her in any case. Whatever Georgina had expected from this Season, it had not included inner turmoil. She had been braced for a variety of problems, but so far, none of these had gone beyond her competence. Treacherously, the attack had come from within. Her own emotions had risen to trouble her, and she was helpless before this unexpected revolution. Susan's pranks paled beside it. Indeed, there were moments when Georgina remembered her fears for Susan with a kind of nostalgia. If only they were her principal worry, she thought at such times. Then, a handsome male face would form in her mind, and she would smile a trifle foolishly.

For her part, Susan Wyndham was feeling dissatisfied and petulant. London was not nearly meeting her expectations. She had had rosy visions of herself as a reigning toast, surrounded by scores of admirers, the indispensable center of a glittering group. And

she had been certain that they would materialize as
soon as she began to go about in society. Instead, she
found she was merely one among many young ladies
being presented, and no one seemed to notice her
special qualities. In particular Baron Ellerton, whom
she had impulsively fastened upon as the object of
her ambitions, paid her no heed whatever. No matter what she did to gain his attention, he either
ignored or circumvented her. For Susan, this was a
novel state of affairs. Her family had always had an
exaggerated respect for her temper, and they had
allowed her much more of her own way than was usual.
Indeed, she was accustomed to being the center of
attention, the one deferred to in making plans and
decisions. She had never considered that this was the
result of her unbridled rages. She had not considered it at all; she had simply assumed it was the
normal state of affairs. Now, in a much larger circle,
among strangers, she found everything changed. No
one deferred, not even William. He was out on his
own most of the time, scarcely ever asking her if she
wished to come or what she would like to do. And
Georgina—here Susan's train of thought paused—
Georgina was an odd case. She certainly never op-
posed Susan's will, but neither did she subordinate
herself to it. It was almost as if, thought Susan, she
lived in some quite different world, in which Susan
was irrelevant.

Naturally, this idea did nothing to improve Susan's
mood. Something, she decided, had to be done. She
would not endure a whole season as merely one of
the mass. But when she tried to think what to do, she
was at a stand. The various schemes that occurred to
her, even she knew to be outrageous. She had no
desire to create a scandal—merely to make her mark.

Looking across the now crowded theater, Susan saw Marianne MacClain enter a box with her mother and Sir Thomas Bentham. She felt a pang of envy. Though she never would admit it, she rather admired Marianne; this was the chief reason for her insistence on their rivalry. It was a way of saying they were alike without the humiliating admission that Susan merely *wished* it were so. Marianne seemed so at ease among the *ton*, and she had an established place in it, of some consequence. All knew her as the girl who had refused a brilliant match, and Susan herself would have given much for such a distinction. But she would not have said this aloud for worlds.

Susan straightened in her chair as Marianne, settled, began to look about the theater, nodding to acquaintances. Susan pretended to have been gazing in quite a different direction, and then to notice her, and bow. She saw William and Tony do likewise, with much more enthusiasm, and Marianne's gentle smile at their changed appearance. Once again, she was racked by jealousy. It was Marianne's ability to laugh at circumstances that filled her with blind rage that impressed Susan the most. Though her family would have been surprised to hear it, Susan was not proud of her temper. It felt to her hardly a part of herself; rather, it was like an inexorable agency descending from outside. Often she said and did things she regretted bitterly later, so bitterly that she refused to acknowledge the fact to anyone. It was less humbling to pretend she had meant it all. But occasionally, as now, she faced the truth. Indeed, such moments had come far more often since she arrived in London.

The play began, breaking off Susan's train of thought. And since she had never seen a play before, she found the spectacle too enthralling to interrupt with gloomy speculations. She sat forward in her chair, arms on the edge of the box, and gave the stage her rapt attention.

Tony was equally fascinated. Indeed, at the first interval, William had some trouble rousing him to visit the boxes. He had to shake his shoulder sharply, as mere words failed to reach him, saying, "Here, what's the matter with you? Are you ill?"

Tony surfaced with a jerk. "What?"

"I asked if you were ill," repeated William. "I've been talking to you for five minutes, and you just sat there looking like a mooncalf. Is it that little blond playing the daughter?" He grinned.

Tony stood, indignant and embarrassed at once. "Nonsense. I was thinking, that's all. Are we going up to the boxes, or not?" He turned away before William could answer, but the latter, seeing his mood, had already chosen silence.

This restraint seemed to mollify Tony, for at the foot of the stairs he asked in a normal tone, "Where to?"

"I ought to pay my respects to Lady Bentham," replied William.

"You mean Marianne," corrected Tony, not averse to getting a little of his own back. "Oh, very well."

Lady Bentham's box already held two visitors, young men whom William eyed with suspicion. But they departed soon after, and the newcomers were free to take the extra chairs and await compliments on their new finery.

Lady Bentham asked whether they liked the play.

They agreed that it was vastly entertaining.

Sir Thomas wondered if this was their first visit to a London theater.

They acknowledged the fact.

Lady Bentham declared that she liked plays above all things, and her husband, in what Tony thought a disgustingly besotted voice, said that this was because she was so sensitive. With this, the Benthams retired into their customary absorption with each other, and Marianne burst out laughing.

Both young men turned to stare at her, frowning, but though she struggled, it was a moment before Marianne regained her composure. At last she managed, "I beg your pardon."

"What's so amusing?" asked Tony suspiciously. He had a sudden awful fear that he looked ridiculous.

"Nothing! That is, your conversation with Mama."

"I must have missed the joke."

Seeing that William, too, was looking thunderous, Marianne suppressed her lingering smile. "It is just that Mama is so woolly-headed lately," she added, as if this explained everything.

The gentlemen puzzled over this briefly, still not certain, but there seemed nothing they could say, and Marianne's next words drove all other thoughts out of their minds.

"You have been to the tailor Sir Thomas suggested, I see."

"Yes," answered Tony eagerly. "What do you think?" He straightened in his chair to give her a good view.

"You are . . . dazzling," said Marianne. "I have never seen such a waistcoat."

"Nor will you," he responded proudly. "The man said this piece of cloth was all he had. Arrived in a special shipment direct from Paris."

"Really? How lucky for you."

Something in her voice made him suspicious again, and he surveyed her for signs of mockery. "It's all the crack."

"I know," agreed Marianne solemnly. "I daresay you will soon be one of the leading lights of the dandy set. Have you met Oliver Grigsby?"

"At the ball the other night." Tony grew confiding. "Actually, it was his coat that decided me on what to buy. I've never seen its like."

Marianne shook her head. "You must tell him so."

"Well, I don't know."

"But he aims to set fashions, Tony. He will be pleased."

Tony pondered this. He had been much taken with the dandy set. Their dress and manners, so different from the older generation's, seemed to express a rebellion akin to his own impulses.

"There's Grigsby now," said William, looking down into the theater.

Tony followed his gaze to the group of budding pinks below. "Perhaps I will just speak to him," he said.

Marianne and William nodded encouragingly, and Tony rose and slipped out of the box with a slight bow to the Benthams.

Immediately, William had qualms. "I suppose it is wrong to push him on them," he said, watching as Tony emerged below and joined Grigsby's group.

"Nonsense. They are harmless."

"Are they?"

"Grigsby and his friends, yes. They are merely young men who enjoy shocking their parents and society with their eccentricities of dress. It lasts only a year or so. I think it is some kind of statement of independence."

"Do you?"

Seeing that he was smiling, Marianne raised her eyebrows.

"You sounded like a dowager giving her judgment of the younger generation," added William.

"I did not!" She drew herself up indignantly, then slowly smiled a little. "Perhaps I have heard someone else say that." Her smile broadened, becoming sheepish. "Mrs. Grigsby, I think."

"A very sensible woman, evidently."

Marianne nodded, and they laughed together.

"And what do you think of *my* new clothes?" asked William then.

"In the very best of taste," she replied promptly.

"You do not think I am making a statement of independence?"

"I don't believe you need to."

Their eyes met, both a bit surprised. Marianne had not known she was going to say that, but once she had, she realized that it was true. William was not much older than Tony, but he was far more sure of himself. For his part, William was pleased as well as startled. Marianne's good opinion was becoming important to him, and he was happy to see that she did not classify him with Tony, whom she clearly viewed as a kind of amusing younger brother.

"Perhaps not," he agreed, holding her eyes. "Indeed, my effort may be just the opposite. My old coat possessed a little *too* much independence."

They laughed together again, each feeling a dawning warmth that intrigued and excited them. But at that moment the warning bell rang, signaling the end of the interval.

"Oh," exclaimed Marianne, her disappointment obvious.

William was pleased to see it, though he cursed all theater managers. He rose, then paused to look down at Marianne. "Perhaps I may call on, er, your mother one day?"

"Yes, of course." She smiled. "I'm sure she would be happy to receive you."

With an answering smile, William turned and strode buoyantly out of the box. Despite the abrupt end to their conversation, he felt quite satisfied with the encounter.

If the second installment of the play seemed less engrossing to certain members of the audience, Susan and Tony did not notice it. Indeed, when the second interval arrived, each was bewitched by the action on stage, and William again had to rouse his friend with a shake. This time Tony said, "By Jove, it is good, isn't it?"

William agreed, though with less fervor. "I'm going up to Susan and Georgina. Coming?"

"Umm? Oh, yes, I suppose I should. How do you think they do it, William?"

"Who? Do what?"

"Actors. I mean, one knows they're playing a role, but I'd swear they mean every word as they say it. It's astonishing."

This was not one of William's areas of expertise. "Well, they have an aptitude, I suppose. And they practice, of course."

Tony nodded. "It's astonishing," he murmured again.

There were no other visitors to the Goring box, and Susan seemed glad to see them. "Isn't the play *wonderful*!" she exclaimed to William as he sat down. "I never imagined it would be like this." Before William could reply, Tony seconded her enthusiasm, and the two at once embarked on a detailed review of the play's action and numerous attractions.

The others watched them, smiling, for a moment; then William said, "Do *you* like it?"

"Yes," responded Georgina. "I think it very well done."

"But you do not fall into raptures."

"Perhaps I am past the age for that."

William had been keeping a surreptitious eye on Marianne across the way, wondering resentfully who the three young men visiting her box might be and whether she was acquainted with all of London, but something in the tone of Georgina's remark drew his full attention. Georgina was looking tired, he saw as he surveyed her more carefully, and her gray eyes showed shadows of some unfamiliar emotion. "Is Susan running you ragged?" he asked quietly. "You mustn't let her, you know. You should ask me for help. I came up to town for that purpose, though I may seem to forget it." He smiled.

"It's all right."

"That I should forget? It isn't. Or do you think I cannot help? You might be surprised."

Georgina looked up, her brown study dispersed finally.

"I've been dealing with Susan almost all my life, you see," added William.

Georgina smiled. "And rather well, I imagine."

He shrugged. "Our brother Nick is better, really. He thinks it out. But I manage. You will ask if you need something, I hope."

She nodded, oddly warmed, and impressed by the inner strength evident in this young man. Whether by temperament or education, he had matured into a calmly capable, quietly compelling man. She could, she realized, rely on him; the thought was comforting.

"You blockhead!" exclaimed Susan, too loudly. "She meant nothing of the kind. She was trying to keep him from seeing that she loved him, so she pretended to be cold."

"Pretended!" retorted Tony, his voice just as penetrating. "She treated him shamefully, and you could tell she didn't care if he went to Italy and died."

"*He* didn't care if she remained behind with her beast of a brother and was made to marry Runyon," Susan snapped. "He didn't mean to do anything about it."

"What could he do? She gave him no sign that he had a right."

"Oh, you are just like him. Any idiot could *see* that—"

"A bit softer, Susan," interrupted Georgina. Their dispute was attracting attention.

Arrested in mid-spate, Susan noticed it. "I was simply trying to explain the play to Tony," she replied with quiet hauteur. "He has misunderstood it completely."

"*I?*" Tony laughed, though he too lowered his voice. "We shall see who has misunderstood when it starts again."

"Yes, we shall," said Susan hotly. They turned their heads ostentatiously away from one another.

William and Georgina exchanged a smile. "Susan, you have not told us if you like our new coats," William pointed out.

But if he thought this placatory, he was mistaken. "You look very well," she replied. "Tony looks a complete quiz."

The latter sputtered with renewed rage. "What do you know about it?" he managed finally. "A chit fresh from a country schoolroom. I shouldn't give a snap of my fingers for *your* opinion if you fell into raptures. Oliver Grigsby said I looked fine as a fivepence."

"Then he must be as silly as you," answered Susan, with that air of utter conviction and infuriating superiority so familiar to her brother.

"He happens to be one of the pinks of the *ton*," responded Tony through gritted teeth.

"A dandy, you mean? Well, that explains it."

Tony looked as if he would cheerfully throttle her. William started to intervene, but the bell rang again, and Tony rose with alacrity to return to his seat. "Miss Goring," he said in his most polished accents, bowing to Georgina. He turned his back on Susan and left the box.

"Idiot," murmured Susan.

"Well, he isn't," William informed her. "And you were dashed rude to him."

"I was rude? What of him?"

"He didn't call you a blockhead."

"He called me a chit!"

Her brother merely looked at her. Gradually Susan's flush lessened. "He made me angry," she said in a subdued voice after a while. "I was so enjoying the play."

"So was he," William pointed out.

"But he was wrong!"

"I understand there may be two opinions on such matters—perhaps even more than two."

Susan tossed her head, started to speak, then changed her mind. "If you do not go, you will miss the end," she said.

William shrugged, smiled at Georgina, and went out. Thus, only Georgina saw Susan's shoulders rise and fall in a great sigh as she leaned forward to watch the resuming play. Georgina was, however, oddly heartened by this reaction.

7

The following afternoon, at the fashionable hour, Susan Wyndham set off to walk in the park, escorted by her maid and the cat Daisy. Susan was not in the best of moods. Neither Georgina nor William had been available when she made up her mind to walk—the former had gone out to Hookham's circulating library and the latter on some unknown errand of his own—and Susan unreasonably took this as a deliberate slight. Actually, her impatience arose out of the fact that she was accustomed to far more exercise than she got in London, for despite her fragile appearance, she habitually rode or walked a goodly distance every day, but she was not aware of this, and so blamed her family for their disregard of her comfort.

Once outside, however, her temper improved. It was a lovely afternoon, and she had put on a new gown of pale green muslin sprigged with tiny darker green flowers and a new chip straw hat. The matching sunshade she raised over her head filled her with deep satisfaction, and an admiring glance from a gentleman on horseback as they entered the park completed her triumph. She lifted her chin and smiled a little, and her maid heaved an almost audible sigh of relief.

Susan chose a path that ran beside the main avenue of the park, where fashionable carriages moved in a dignified cavalcade to allow their passengers to bow to one another and exchange occasional remarks. She kept a sharp eye on these vehicles, hoping to see an acquaintance, but only twice did she spy a known face, and on the second occasion the rider did not notice her.

This ruffled Susan's temper again. It was exactly as she had concluded at the theater, she told herself irritably: she wasn't enough known to make a hit. Grandmama had promised a ball in her honor, but since she had fallen ill the plan had not been mentioned. Georgina was clearly incapable of carrying through, and even Susan was a little daunted at the idea of supervising such an undertaking. Yet her introduction to society so far had been definitely disappointing. Susan watched the passing stream of carriages, filled with elegant people whom she did not recognize, and felt suddenly isolated and excluded. She was prettier and more interesting than any of those women, she thought petulantly. Why should they have every advantage and she none at all!

With this very unfair observation, Susan turned homeward. She was not consciously aware of the need to relieve her pent-up feelings in some outburst, but she knew she strongly wished to talk with William or Georgina.

It was at this moment that Susan saw Baron Ellerton approaching from the direction of the park gates. He was driving an impeccable high-perch phaeton drawn by the most magnificent team of chestnuts Susan had ever seen, and he handled these obviously spirited animals with negligent grace. Without pausing to think, Susan stepped forward, nearly into the carriageway, smiled, and raised her hand. When it seemed as if the baron would simply bow politely and drive on, she moved even further forward, eliciting a warning exclamation from her maid. Susan continued to smile.

Ellerton pulled up with a mixture of annoyance and amusement. The Wyndham chit was certainly determined, he thought as he brought the phaeton to a halt beside her. He had never encountered such a strong will in such a deceptive package, but if she thought to get the best of him, she was mistaken. The baron had been a target for countless marriage-minded young ladies and gimlet-eyed mothers in the fifteen years he had been on the town, and he had profited from this experience. "Good day, Miss Wyndham," he said coolly. "A fine day for a stroll."

"Oh, I should much rather be driving," replied Susan brightly. "*Would* you be so kind as to take me up for a spin round the park, Baron Ellerton? I have never ridden in a phaeton in my life." She gazed up at him with large innocent eyes, just as if this were not an outrageous request. Both her maid and the middle-aged groom who sat beside the baron gasped.

Ellerton had not counted on such effrontery. He could deal with simpering, flirtation, even tears, with the greatest ease, but Susan's flat demand—for it amounted to that—could not be turned aside without absolute rudeness, and this Baron Ellerton found himself incapable of voicing. His handsome face stiff with annoyance, he answered, "Very well, Miss Wyndham. You may get down, Hines."

Any other young lady in London would have cringed at his tone, and hastily withdrawn her suggestion, but Susan merely turned to her maid and said, "You may go, Lucy. I daresay the baron will escort me home later."

Lucy opened her mouth and closed it like a beached fish.

"Oh, and I will take Daisy's basket. He loves carriage rides."

The maid, knowing this to be utterly untrue, paled and tried again to speak. But no words came as Susan took the basket from her nerveless fingers and accepted the groom's aid in climbing up the vehicle's steps. Only when the phaeton was moving away did she regain her powers of speech, responding to the groom Hines's "Well, I never!" with a half-hysterical catalog of the vicissitudes of her post. Hines was forced to support her on the journey home, giving her gratefully into the hands of the cook, who had witnessed such scenes before.

"This is splendid," declared Susan as she settled herself in the carriage. She set Daisy's basket beside her feet and adjusted her dark green shawl about her shoulders. The view from the phaeton's high seat was impressive; she felt far above the park saunterers, whom she had numbered among just moments ago.

The complacency in her expression goaded the baron, and now that there were no listeners, he felt able to remark, "You know, Miss Wyndham, it is not usual for a young lady to command a gentleman with whom she is barely acquainted to take her up in his carriage."

"I know," agreed Susan. "But I didn't think you would ask *me*, and I so wanted to come."

Once again, Ellerton found himself silenced by her bluntness. One side of his mouth quirking up at the ridiculousness of it, he began, "Nonetheless—"

But Susan did not wish to hear his admonitions. "And everyone will see me and talk of it," she interrupted happily. "It is quite a mark of distinction to be driven by you."

The baron was not unaware of this. "A mark of distinction is customarily *bestowed*, Miss Wyndham," he answered dryly, "not, er, seized."

"Yes. But you have no idea how difficult it is to make an impression here in London. There are so many girls coming out, and even though they are mostly the merest nothings, one is classified with them and ignored. I want to make a splash!"

"I see."

"Oh, I don't wish to do anything scandalous." She turned wide green eyes on his face. "But I *should* be a famous belle, Baron Ellerton."

Taking in her passionate determination, Ellerton found his annoyance fading into curiosity. Irritating, Miss Wyndham certainly was, but she was also genuinely unusual. Moreover, she had a point. Though there were many factors involved in the creation of a reigning toast—money and rank as well and beauty and personality—a strong character such as this girl clearly possessed often tipped the scales. Ellerton discovered an interest in her future career, though no desire to take an active role in it. Indeed, the thought made him shudder. But he would enjoy observing her tactics. At the moment, however, he had a more important concern. "Perhaps," he conceded. "But I shall not be used in your campaign again, Miss Wyndham. I give you fair warning, the next time you put me in such a position, I shall be rude, as I was not today."

She did not pretend to misunderstand him. "I'm sorry. I won't do it again."

The baron glanced at her face. She was grinning mischievously but seemed sincere. "See that you don't," he finished, stifling a laugh.

Susan nodded. "Now that that is settled," she added, "could I take the reins for a little while?"

Ellerton stared at her as if she had gone mad.

"I am a famous whip," she assured him. "I drive a great deal in the country. I have even handled a team."

"No one drives my horses but me," he replied in his most repressive accents.

"But I—"

"Miss Wyndham! We have just discussed your behavior. I tell you now that this is absolutely beyond the line. You cannot drive my cattle!" To himself he was marveling at her daring. No *man* in London would have asked this, but she did so without the least sign of constraint.

Susan's elfin features set in lines that would have warned anyone better acquainted with her, and she began to look about the park as if plotting strategy. Actually, she did not understand exactly what she had asked. Her brothers had always allowed her to try their horses; William was a bruising rider but lacked finesse, and Nicholas preferred scholarly pursuits to a neck-or-nothing gallop. Their mounts were far gentler than those Baron Ellerton bred, and because Susan could best either of the Wyndham men, she had an inflated idea of her own competence. To her, Ellerton's refusal seemed simply a punishment for her earlier behavior. "I suppose I should be going home now," Susan declared in a deceptively mild tone as they approached the gate of the park once more.

"Certainly," the baron agreed, only too pleased to

cut his drive short if it meant ridding himself of her. He maneuvered around a dawdling barouche and turned into the street.

Susan leaned over and checked the lid on Daisy's basket. As she opened it a crack, the cat's broad ginger head thrust out, his yellow eyes glittering with malice. Daisy was not fond of carriage rides, but if forced to ride, he much preferred sitting up where he could see, or at the very least being free to move about. Shut in his stuffy basket, which he at all times hated, and bounced about by the vehicle, he had nursed a towering rage. At the first sign of rescue, he was out of the container and standing rigid on the floor of the phaeton. Susan, who might have been expected to know his predilections, merely gazed at him speculatively.

"Your cat must stay in the basket," ordered Ellerton, glancing briefly down, then up again. The busy London streets required all his attention.

With the look of a dispassionate experimenter, Susan advanced one kid-shod foot to prod Daisy's stomach sharply.

The cat went up like a rocket, teeth bared, claws outstretched. The latter sank into the immaculate yellow pantaloons that sheathed the baron's leg and held there while Daisy yowled defiance. Then, like lightning, he began to climb.

Ellerton swore, his hands dropping for a startled instant. The team increased its pace, barely skirting an overladen cart slowing before a greengrocer's. "Get that creature off me!" he commanded through gritted teeth.

Susan bit her lower lip. "Oh dear," she said in an insincere voice.

"I said . . ." Daisy reached the baron's knee, paused,

then leapt, claws extended, for his chest. Ellerton desperately gathered the reins in one hand and sought to capture the animal with the other.

"Look out for that gig," cried Susan.

The baron attempted to pull up the phaeton, collar Daisy, and glare furiously at Susan all at once. The cat, fighting, as he thought, for life, limb, and freedom, wrapped himself about Ellerton's neck and tried to shred his very elegant neckcloth. The baron cursed fluently again.

Susan, seeing the opportunity she had been awaiting, seized the phaeton's reins from its owner's momentarily slack grasp, slapped them across the team's glossy backs, and laughed as the carriage began to race through the cobbled streets.

The baron shouted something incoherent, but Susan's unexpected move had thrown him back in his seat and driven Daisy to an absolute frenzy of rage. As he tried to regain his balance, the cat swarmed about his head, hissing and scratching and requiring all his attention.

Susan realized almost at once that she had made a dreadful mistake. The baron's team was far less tractable that any she had driven before. Indeed, it took all her strength merely to keep hold of the reins. Any thought of controlling the chestnuts had to be abandoned. The phaeton raced at a dangerous speed through the streets, eliciting angry shouts and leaving a wake of shaken pedestrians and, in at least one case, scattered vegetables. Holding on with all her might, Susan soon began to be truly frightened. She dared a glance at the baron. He was trying to throttle Daisy, who was fighting back with all his wiles. "Daisy, stop it!" she cried. But the cat was too far gone to hear by now.

They hurtled out into a broad highway, the team turning of its own accord and racing along it. Susan's wrists ached, and the wind of their passage had whirled away her beloved sunshade and torn her hat to dangle from its ribbons at her back. The buildings were thinning, she noticed. They must be near the edge of town.

With a jerk, Ellerton got both hands round Daisy's squirming body and threw the cat from the carriage into a tree beside the road. At once he turned to grasp the reins, and Susan gave them up without protest. Indeed, she was only too glad to relinquish responsibility for their disastrous course.

But this new disturbance was too much for Ellerton's high-spirited team. Never in their pampered lives had they endured such treatment. They had always been driven with impeccable skill and received in the city streets or country lanes with deference and admiration. These violent jerks on their guiding lines and shouts and curses from all sides had upset their high-bred equilibrium. As the baron strove with all his strength to pull them up and stop the phaeton, all four rebelled, galloping even faster than before.

Seeing blood beginning to fleck the froth at the corners of the horse's mouths, Ellerton eased his grip, letting them run. "I won't ruin them," he snapped at Susan. "They will have to run it out."

She simply nodded, white and ashamed, but less frightened now that he had taken over.

The chestnuts strained in their harness for nearly half an hour, pulling the tossing phaeton through ruts and dust, heedless of anything but their need to flee. Ellerton held the reins with iron wrists, gradually reestablishing control and very slowly moderating their pace. They were well outside London when it at last appeared that he would be able to stop the carriage, and he felt free to glance at Susan and open his mouth for a blistering setdown. At that moment, a pair of sparrows erupted from the bushes at the right of the road and hurtled across under the very noses of the leaders. The chestnuts shied violently, and one of the leaders reared, then plunged into the foliage. The phaeton rose perilously on one wheel, hanging there for an endless instant, then slammed to the ground, flinging both passengers from their seats into the leaves.

Susan landed on a thorn bush, the breath quite knocked out of her. As she strove for air, thorns prickled her from all sides, but the pain was nothing to her apprehension about what the baron would do to her when he found her. He was furious, and she had to acknowledge, he had every right to be. Her dreadful temper had gotten the better of her again.

Susan considered trying to crawl away through the bushes and make her own way back to London, but her sense of responsibility at last forced her to struggle out of the thorns, leaving a good many scraps of sprigged muslin behind her, and return to the road. She saw the phaeton at once; it lay on its side and would not move again without repair. The team was still harnessed to it. They were standing still, sweating and trembling in the traces. She should try to cut them loose, Susan realized, but when she ventured closer, the more nervous leader shied again and looked as if he would lash out with his hooves. Better leave them to the baron, Susan thought, backing away again. And she frowned as she looked about for him. Surely he would have gone directly to his horses?

Frightened again, Susan returned to the bushes

and began to search, calling Ellerton's name. There was no response, which shook her further. She plunged through the undergrowth, oblivious of lashing branches and thorns, until at last she came upon him, on his back under an elm, white and unmoving.

With a cry, she sank to her knees at his side. There was a great gash in the other side of his forehead, she saw at once. It had bled all down the side of his face and dyed the fallen leaves beneath crimson. Too, one of his legs lay at an odd angle.

Some girls might have fallen into a fit of the vapors then and there, but Susan was made of stronger stuff. She had seen a number of hunting accidents, and knew something about treating such injuries. Cuts to the head always bled heavily, she knew. Nonetheless, her hands were shaking as she groped in the baron's pocket for a handkerchief to bind up the wound. She then felt for his pulse, conscious of an almost unbearable relief when she found it, and ran her hands along the bent leg. Ellerton groaned when she touched it, and she snatched her hand away.

"Baron Ellerton," she said urgently. "Baron!"

He groaned again but did not wake. Susan sat back on her heels, still trembling, and wondered how best to find help. She would have to leave him, she decided, while she walked along the road to the closest house or village. She ran back to the phaeton, and after a rapid search, found a rug, which she hurried to spread over him. The horses shied again as she passed. Then, hair wild and bleeding from numerous thorn pricks, Susan set off toward town.

8

At nearly the same time, Georgina Goring went in search of Susan's brother. She found him in the library, dozing over a book in the hour before dinner. "William," she said softly, and he started awake.

"Uuh! What? Oh, Georgina." He straightened in the brown leather armchair.

"William, do you remember you said I should ask for your help if I needed it?"

Her tone made him rub the last drowsiness from his eyes. "Of course. Is something wrong?"

"I hope not." She hesitated. "I am worried about Susan."

He groaned. "What's she done now?"

Georgina sighed and sank down on the sofa nearby. "Perhaps nothing. But I can't help but be concerned." She told William the maid Lucy's story. "It is nearly two hours since then, and she is not back," she finished. "I don't know what can have happened."

Some men might have doubted the baron's motives or suspected him of treachery. William Wyndham exclaimed, "She has kidnapped him!" and put his head in his hands.

Georgina was torn between laughter and outrage. "William! Why should she do any such thing?"

"Why does Susan do anything?" he retorted, raising his head again. "He probably gave her a well-deserved setdown for pushing herself upon him, and she decided to make him sorry."

This sounded disturbingly plausible to Georgina. "But how could she—"

"Susan would find a way," interrupted William positively.

Once again, Georgina could not muster convincing arguments against him, and her spirits fell even further. She had failed in her duties as a chaperon, she thought, just as she feared she would. But she also felt a spark of resentment. That Susan should disappear in the company of Baron Ellerton seemed to her unfair, though she would have been hard put to explain what exactly that meant. She pushed these thoughts aside. "We must look for her," she told William.

He nodded wearily. "I'll get my horse and ride through the park. Of course, they can't still be there."

"I'll speak to Lucy again. Perhaps she will remember something Susan said, or . . ." She trailed off, and they gazed at one another helplessly, each feeling that their suggestions were weak. Then William shrugged and went out.

The maid had no more information, and William returned as the sky was darkening toward evening with no news, though he had ridden along all the streets leading to the park and even gone to inquire at Baron Ellerton's house. He had been turned away with some hauteur by the butler, whose icy reserve was such an effective mask of his concern that William never suspected it.

"What do we do now?" he asked when he and Georgina had left the dinner table, having eaten very little.

She rubbed her eyes. "I don't know. I suppose I must speak to Aunt Sybil, but . . ."

"It might make her worse. I could go and fetch Christopher, but that would take three days." He frowned.

Georgina found his confidence in his stepfather touching, but unhelpful. "No, we shall have to think of something ourselves," she concluded.

They looked at each other, their feelings very similar. Georgina was scolding herself for her inadequacy as a guide to Susan, and William was deploring his poor showing as head of the Wyndham family. Both had a strong sense of responsibility and a hatred of failure.

"I *could* go back to the baron's house and tell the truth," ventured William, sounding far from eager.

"No. We must keep this a secret as long as we can. I even managed to fob Lucy off, for a while. It mustn't get out."

"What mustn't?" inquired a cheerful voice from the drawing-room doorway, and they turned to find Tony Brinmore and Marianne MacClain standing there.

Their surprise and chagrin were so obvious that Marianne said, "A footman let us in, and told us you were here. We were passing by on our way home from the Wigginses', and Tony wished to speak to William. We would not have come up if . . ."

"What mustn't get out?" repeated Tony, throwing himself into an armchair and gazing at William with cheerful curiosity.

"Tony, we should go," responded Marianne.

He looked startled. "We just got here. What's the matter with—?"

The maid Lucy rushed in, wringing her hands.

"Oh, Miss Georgina, the cat's come home," she cried, oblivious of the presence of visitors. "All dusty and draggled, he is, with a cut on his leg. It's footpads, or highwaymen, I'll lay my life. Miss Susan's killed. Or worse!" She began to blubber noisily.

"You mean she took the cat with her!" exclaimed William, astounded.

Lucy was incapable of speech. Georgina closed her eyes and prayed for strength. "What's Susan done now?" asked Tony, clearly intrigued and amused.

Marianne tugged at his arm. "Tony, come on. We are in the way here."

He shook her off. "Nonsense. William needs my help."

Marianne looked at Georgina, who had gone to deal with Lucy. "I do beg your pardon," she said.

Georgina simply shook her head. She succeeded in quieting Lucy enough to guide her out of the room and down to the kitchen, where the cook again took over ministrations. When she returned to the drawing room, she found William completing the tale of the day's events. "So we don't know where she's gone. But now that I hear about Daisy, I have a good idea."

"Where?" Georgina exclaimed, too eager to scold him for spreading the tale.

William turned. "Ellerton's killed her," he replied matter-of-factly. "Throttled her and left her under a bush in the park. Daresay he tried for Daisy, too, but that animal is devilishly clever."

Tony burst out laughing. Marianne, throwing him an indignant look, went to Georgina. "I am terribly sorry. I . . ."

"It's all right. I know you will not talk of it." Georgina turned to Tony. "And if you do, you will—"

"What do you take me for?" Tony was still fighting a smile. "I mean to help."

With a deep sigh, Georgina went to sit on the sofa again. Marianne joined her. "I don't see what any of us can do. We don't know where to search."

"Perhaps the cat can lead us to them," suggested Tony, grinning.

"Oh, stop it!" responded Marianne. "This is no joking matter."

"Do you suppose there has been an accident?" wondered Georgina. "Lucy said it was a high-perch phaeton. They don't look very safe."

"Ellerton is one of the finest whips in the country," said Marianne. "I can't imagine him taking a spill."

"Susan would," declared William. "And she'd be wild to take the ribbons."

"Ellerton would never allow it," Marianne assured him.

"No."

They sat in glum silence for a while, each trying to think of some plan, and none succeeding. Georgina was growing desperate when the butler entered with an envelope. "For you, miss," he said. "A boy just brought it."

They all clustered around as she opened it and scanned the message. "Oh, my God!" said William then, collapsing into a chair.

"She's killed *him*," crowed Tony. "Or half-killed him, anyhow."

Marianne was silent, but Georgina crumpled the paper in her fist and said, "I must go to them at once," her voice shaking.

No one disagreed, but Marianne surveyed the other woman with deep concern. She could see that Georgina was dreadfully upset, and she understood at least some of the reasons. "I will go with you," she offered.

"We'll all go," said Tony, not quite able to hide his excitement at the adventure. "You'll need someone to, er, run errands and, er, that sort of thing."

In the end, despite William's protests and Georgina's firm denials, they all set out together, Marianne and Georgina in Lady Goring's chaise and the young men riding. By the time they had gathered their things and sent word to Marianne's mother, it was full dark, and they had to travel very slowly. Gradually, even Tony's high spirits were dampened by the dismal drive, and conversation dropped to nothing.

Susan had long since decided that this was the worst day of her life. After leaving the wrecked phaeton, she walked nearly half an hour before reaching a cluster of buildings. And when she came among them, she saw to her chagrin that they all belonged to one of the main posting houses on the road out of London. The place bustled with ostlers, waiters, and elegant travelers, and she drew a great many curious looks as she made her way inside, her tattered gown and tangled hair making her feel horribly self-conscious. With every step she expected to be recognized and questioned by some London acquaintance, but mercifully she managed to find the innkeeper and tell her story without being remarked.

At this point, she began to appreciate her luck, for the landlord at once delegated three of his large staff to drive her back to the phaeton and help her bring Ellerton to the inn. He sent another for the nearest doctor and ordered one of the maids to lend Susan her shawl. Amidst this whirlwind of activity,

Susan at first felt dazed, then grateful to have some of the responsibility taken from her shoulders.

She guided the men back to the location of the accident, where a small huddle of onlookers had by this time collected. As two of these were examining the equipage with furtive greed, Susan was unexpectedly thankful for the horses' difficult temperament. They had clearly kept everyone away from the phaeton. "He is in here," she told the men, and they pushed through the foliage to the baron, who lay as she had left him, still unconscious.

"Be careful of his leg," she warned as they transferred him to an improvised stretcher. "Oh, shouldn't he have wakened by now?"

"He do look bad," replied one of the men, an ostler. "That were quite a spill you took." His tone was almost admiring, but it did nothing to comfort Susan.

They laid Ellerton in the wagon they had brought, and the ostler went to deal with the team. "They are in a bad temper," warned Susan, but he merely gave her a gap-toothed grin and began to murmur to the animals. By the time the wagon was turned and ready to depart, he had gotten close enough to stroke the noses of the leaders.

"I'll have to lead 'em back," he called. "Axle's broken. I'll cut 'em loose and be along directly."

The wagon driver nodded, and they went slowly back to the posting house. Susan sat in back to watch over Ellerton, but though he groaned once or twice when the wheels jolted over something in the road, he did not come round.

By the time they had carried him up to one of the inn's bedrooms, the doctor had arrived. Susan was ordered from the room and forced to wait in a parlor downstairs while he made his examination. Here, for the first time able to relax a little, she nearly gave way to tears. This time her wretched temper had gotten her into a scrape she might not escape unscathed, she thought miserably. She had meant no harm—or not much, at least—but she had again allowed her fury to take over, with disastrous results. What if he died? she wondered. What would she do?

Shuddering, she wrapped her arms around her chest and went to stand by the window, staring unseeing out at the approaching dusk. Her supposed admiration for Baron Ellerton was forgotten in worry for herself; he was to her at that moment less a man than a symbol of her own mistakes and stupidity. If he is all right, she told herself fervently, I promise I will change. I will never do such a foolish thing again as long as I live.

"Miss?" said a deep scratchy voice from the doorway.

Susan started and turned. "Doctor! Is he . . . how is he?"

"Not good." The doctor came further into the room. He was a dark, competent-looking man of about forty. "His leg is broken, as you thought, as well as two ribs. But it is the blow to the head that worries me. He obviously struck something very hard when he was thrown from the carriage. He still has not regained consciousness."

"Does that mean . . . will he . . . ?" Susan's mouth was very dry, and she found she could not ask the crucial question.

"I cannot tell anything for certain until he wakes," answered the doctor seriously. "You must send for me as soon as he does. I will come back in the morning in any case."

She nodded, numb.

The doctor eyed her, pity and uncertainty in his brown eyes. "Is there someone you can send for? You should be in bed yourself. Are you sure you're all right?"

"Perfectly." She didn't look it as she gazed abstract-edly about the room. She would have to write to Georgina and William, she thought.

"You are . . . that is, the gentleman is a member of your family?"

"Oh, no. We were just . . . out driving."

"I see."

His tone made Susan focus on him again. "The horses were frightened and bolted," she added. "We . . . he said they must run themselves out. We came from London." The doctor's expression told Susan how improbable this sounded, but she refused to tell a stranger about her dangerous prank. Gathering the shreds of her dignity, she continued, "Thank you very much for your help. I must write to my family now."

This seemed to relieve him somewhat. "Good. I will see you in the morning, then." His cheeks red-dened slightly. "Or, that is, I will see the gentleman, and whoever stays with him. My name is Mason, by the way." He paused, waiting for Susan to give her name.

She balked. This escapade would cause storms of gossip if word of it got out. "Thank you very much for your help, Dr. Mason," she answered dismissively.

He stiffened a little, then bowed and went out.

Susan put her face in her hands and stood very still for a long moment, then straightened and moved to the writing desk in the corner of the parlor. For the first time in her life she longed for William's down-to-earth advice. He would be furious with her—rightly, she admitted—but he could stand by her and do whatever he could to help her out of this tangle. As would Georgina, Susan realized. Though her hand trembled as she scribbled a note to them, she was also filled with a warm flood of relief.

9

Georgina and the others arrived at the posting house very late that night. Susan had gone up to her bedchamber, but she had not undressed, being certain sleep was impossible. Thus, when Georgina tapped very lightly at the door, she answered at once, and immediately flung herself into Georgina's startled embrace. "Thank heaven you have come! I feared you would wait until morning. I have gone nearly distracted trying to think what to do."

Georgina patted her back comfortingly and waited a moment to let her regain her composure. Then she said, "How is Baron Ellerton? And what happened, Susan? Your note said only that he was injured."

Susan stepped back a pace and hung her head. "He is very bad. The landlady is sitting with him now. It is all my fault, but I am sorry!" This last rose into a wail.

"But what happened?" Georgina was sympathetic but impatient.

"I saw the baron in the park," began Susan in a small voice.

"Yes, we know about that. Lucy told us. But I think we had better go down to the others. That way you needn't tell the story but once."

"What others? Is William with you? Of course, he would be."

Georgina nodded. "And Lady Marianne MacClain and Mr. Brinmore."

Susan stared at her, appalled.

"They called just as we received your letter," added Georgina, conscious that Susan had some right to be upset. "They came upon William and me before we realized, and heard part of the story. Then Lucy grew hysterical, and . . . there was nothing for it but to tell them the whole."

Susan recovered from her frozen astonishment. "I cannot possibly face them, Georgina. I won't go down!"

"They have been very kind," protested the other. "They want to help."

"Help! Marianne will gloat over my foolishness. She probably came only because of the baron. And Tony will laugh himself sick. I will not see them!"

"Nonsense!" insisted Georgina. "All of us are here to help. Come." She took Susan's arm and attempted to lead her, but the younger girl pulled away. It was nearly twenty minutes before she could be convinced to descend to the parlor where the others waited, and even then she did so with no good grace.

Tony and William were lounging on a sofa when they entered, half-asleep. Marianne sat opposite, looking tired but determinedly alert.

"Hello," said Susan, stepping into the room ahead of Georgina. "Isn't this the most ridiculous muddle? But you needn't all have come out here. Things are nearly under control again." She took the remaining armchair and looked from one to another of them, smiling.

Georgina couldn't help but gape. Susan seemed a

wholly different person from the frightened young girl upstairs.

"What the deuce have you done, Susan?" asked William. "Is Ellerton badly hurt?"

His sister looked solemn. "Yes, I fear he is. I have been very foolish." But her tone showed none of the anguished contrition she had exhibited only minutes earlier. "I tried to drive his team, you see, and—"

"Ellerton allowed you to drive his horses?" interrupted Marianne, amazed.

"Well, no." Slowly she told them the story. She would have preferred to omit certain details, but the others asked questions which forced her to reveal them. There was no other explanation for what had happened.

At the description of Daisy's attack, Tony choked with laughter, and even Georgina was forced to bite her lip to keep back a smile. "That hellish animal is all right, by the by," added William. "He found his way back to the house."

"Did he?" Susan was admiring, and diverted from her tale. "How clever he is." She avoided Marianne's outraged gaze. The latter was stunned that Susan had used her previous scheme for this.

"Too clever by half," growled her brother. "What happened then?"

She described the accident and its aftermath. "The doctor will call in the morning," she concluded. "He hopes the baron may be better then."

This reduced them to glum silence again. Ellerton's precarious state weighed on all their minds.

"So, what are we going to do?" asked William. Instinctively he looked to Georgina, though he would have denied any claim that he expected her to save the situation.

"We must see what the doctor says," she answered, looking fatigued and distressed. "And we must see that he is well nursed, of course. We will have to send word to his family." She turned to Marianne. "Do you know them?"

The girl frowned. "I don't think he has any close relations. I have never heard of any."

"Well, we will inform his household. They will know."

"But what are we going to tell them?" wondered William.

This was the difficult question. They all contemplated it for a moment.

"We can't give out the true story," he added then. "It would create a scandal." He glared at Susan, who avoided his eyes.

Georgina pondered. "We will let it be known that Baron Ellerton has had a carriage accident," she said. "Susan will not come into it. And we will see that he is cared for." She paused. "If he has no suitable family, I will nurse him myself."

"You?" William was surprised. "Susan should do it, if anyone." But he eyed his sister doubtfully.

"I doubt that nursing is one of her talents," responded Georgina, and no one disagreed. "It is, however, one of mine. I nursed my father through his last illness." She did not add that the thought of allowing anyone else to care for Ellerton annoyed her intensely. "The rest of you will return to London and go on as before."

"You cannot stay here alone," objected Marianne.

"I will send for my maid. And I imagine some of Ellerton's servants will come to help. I shan't be alone."

"But it isn't fair."

Georgina shrugged.

"I shan't be able to go on as before without you to chaperon me," pointed out Susan with diffidence. She felt that this might annoy them, yet it was important to her.

"William can escort you," said Georgina.

"But . . ."

"You can go about with me, if you like," offered Marianne, her tone barely warm. She was not feeling in charity with Susan Wyndham.

"Good," replied Georgina, as if all were settled. Susan looked skeptical.

"But how will we explain your absence?" asked William. "*And* your presence here? If we have Ellerton's servants, they will spread the tale."

This caused another silence.

"It is easy enough to tell people I have been called away," said Georgina meditatively. "We must tell Aunt Sybil and your mother the truth, of course." She paused. "Ellerton's servants will not know me."

"But travelers passing through this inn may," put in Marianne.

"Umm. Well, I will simply have to keep to my room."

"Ellerton'll have visitors," protested William. "This won't work, Georgina. I say we just hire a nurse and—"

She shook her head. "You cannot trust hired nurses. Some are good, but others . . . I learned with my father that one must be on hand oneself."

"Tell them you stopped at this inn on your way, er, somewhere, and found Ellerton here. Took pity on him," suggested Tony, who had contributed nothing so far. "No one else to watch over him, so you stayed."

"That would never work," scoffed Marianne.

"Why not?"

They all contemplated the idea for a moment.

"It *might* do," admitted William. "You could repeat what you told us about nurses. Say you had a particularly poor specimen with your father—"

"Which we *did*," interjected Georgina.

"And you couldn't just leave him in the hands of such a person." William seemed to warm to his story as he went on.

"You tried to send for his family, but there was no one to come," contributed Marianne.

"Very awkward, of course, but what could you do?" finished Tony, very proud of his scheme.

For some reason, the possibility that her plan would work filled Georgina with joy. "Good! Very good. That should pass muster. There will be talk, naturally, but . . ."

"It is unfair that they should talk about you rather than me," objected Susan, her conscience pricking her through her relief.

"It certainly is," agreed her brother, "but I see no way around it. And it won't be that same sort of talk. Besides, Georgina is . . ." He stopped and flushed.

"Ten years older than you," finished Georgina calmly. "Quite on the shelf, in fact. I daresay the gossip will die down almost at once."

None of them disputed this, but all four looked uncomfortable.

"Well, now that that is settled," Georgina continued, "we should all try to sleep. There will be a great deal to do in the morning. William, did you speak to the landlord about rooms?"

"Yes. That's all right."

"Splendid. Let us go up, then." She turned, and Tony rose to follow, but the others hesitated.

"I say, Georgina," blurted William, "this is really good of you. I don't know how . . . Isn't it, Susan?" He scowled at his sister to hide a softer emotion.

Susan nodded vigorously.

"Indeed, it is . . . thoroughly admirable," agreed Marianne.

"Stuff!" replied Georgina, and walked out into the hallway.

None of them slept particularly well, and in the morning there were notes to be written and arrangements to be made. Georgina took some trouble over the composition of her letter to Baron Ellerton's household, knowing that whatever tale she told was likely to be circulated throughout London. "You will be responsible for speaking to our own servants," she told William when she gave it to him. "Their knowledge is garbled and incomplete, but they should be asked not to speak of the incident in the park."

"Of course," said William.

"Susan, here is a list of the things I shall need. You can pack them up for me and send them down with Lucy." It had been decided that Susan and Georgina would exchange maids, to remove Lucy from London and the temptations of gossip.

"We'll all be at your service for errands and the like," offered Tony. "You need only call."

"I shall." Georgina smiled. "And now, you should be on your way. That note should be delivered as soon as possible."

The chaise had already been ordered. The four young people gathered their things, and Georgina walked with them to the wide front door. Outside, Tony and William mounted up, but the girls lingered.

"I feel as if we were abandoning you," said Marianne, holding out her hand. "Are you certain you do not want one of us to stay?"

"Completely," responded Georgina. "It would not do." She smiled. She had been greatly impressed with Marianne's calm good sense and ready sympathy through this episode. Susan might actually be better off under her tutelage, she had decided.

"If you change your mind, you need only write," said the other.

Georgina nodded, still smiling, and Marianne turned to climb into the chaise.

This left only Susan. "I feel dreadfully guilty," she said in a low voice. "You are paying the price for my folly."

"You may make it up by falling into no more scrapes," replied Georgina.

"I shan't. I shall be a model of propriety."

This made Georgina smile again. "Don't promise what you cannot fulfill. I will be content if you are merely a little prudent."

Susan bridled, then grinned, her elfin face lighting with mischief. "Very well. I think I can manage that."

Georgina laughed. "Good! Now, go."

Susan got into the chaise, and the party set off. Georgina stayed to wave, then turned back to her duties. She felt a curious sense of relief to be rid of her family and friends. Though she would not have said it aloud, she found she relished the idea of a time of solitude, with worthwhile work to do. It was much more to her taste than the gaieties of the Season. She did not explore her emotions beyond this, and thus was not required to consider the pleasure she took in the thought of caring for Baron Ellerton. She was terribly concerned for him. She had visited his room twice during the night, and each time the landlady had shaken her head and whispered that he had not come round. Georgina's deep anxiety was at least partially eased by the knowledge that she would be doing her utmost to help him.

Dr. Mason arrived soon after this, and Georgina received him just outside Ellerton's room. When she had introduced herself and explained that she would be nursing the patient, the doctor was relieved. This clear-eyed young woman seemed much better suited to the task than the shaken girl he had met yesterday. "You are a member of his family?" he asked.

"No. Unfortunately he has none. I am a friend who happened to be traveling and found him here. I have had some experience with hired nurses and will not leave him to them."

"Ah, you have worked in a sickroom yourself, perhaps?" he was examining her measuringly.

"My father's. And I will have the help of my maid and, I think, some of the baron's servants."

"Baron, is he?" Mason nodded. It had been obvious to him that his patient was distinguished. It was also obvious that he was not being told the whole story, but he was not surprised by this.

"Baron Ellerton. And my name is Georgina Goring. Will you examine him now? I am very worried."

"Of course." Dr. Mason disappeared into the bedchamber, impressed anew with Miss Goring's capable air.

His expression was less cheerful when he came out again, and in answer to Georgina's inquiring look, he shook his head. "I don't like it. I wish he would wake. I can make no final judgment on his state until he does."

"Is there no sign when that may happen?" Her voice trembled slightly.

"No. In some of these cases . . ." He hesitated.

"What?"

Dr. Mason shrugged. "Sometimes, a person taking a blow to the head never wakes. He simply . . . fades away."

"That will not happen to Baron Ellerton!" exclaimed Georgina. The doctor raised his eyebrows at her vehemence, and she quickly added, "Is there nothing I can do to help him?"

"Try to make him drink. Speak to him now and then." She nodded as if memorizing these meager instructions, and the doctor wished he could offer more. "I'll call again this afternoon," he finished, putting on his hat. "Send for me if there is a change before that."

"I will."

Mason took his leave, and Georgina slipped back into the bedchamber that was to be the focus of her existence for an indefinite time. The blinds were half drawn so that it was dim. A single candle stood on the bedside table, screened so as not to shine in Ellerton's eyes. He lay as he had ever since Georgina arrived, on his back, unmoving, his breath now shallow, now rasping. She moved closer and scanned his chalk-white skin and bloodless lips. The innkeeper had removed his clothes and put him into one of his own nightshirts last night when the doctor set the broken bones. Since then, there had been no change. She leaned over him. "Baron Ellerton," she said in clear tones. "Baron, can you hear me? Wake up."

There was no reaction. His eyes remained closed, and he neither moved nor made a sound, though occasionally in the night he had groaned, she knew. With a sigh, Georgina settled herself in the armchair drawn up on the other side of the small table. It was frustrating not to be able to do more, but she would follow the doctor's instructions and wait. She refused to allow the smallest doubt of his recovery to enter her mind.

The morning passed slowly. Georgina read one of the dog-eared periodicals a traveler had left behind at the inn and looked forward to the arrival of her own things. Then, at least, she would have books and sewing to fill her time. She ate luncheon downstairs, the landlady again sitting with Ellerton, and was starting upstairs once more when the sounds of an arrival drew her to the parlor window in hopes her luggage had come.

It had not. She had never seen the very elegant traveling carriage drawn up outside, and she was about to turn away when her attention was caught by its occupant, who was just climbing down.

He did not look like the vehicle's owner. He was a small bandy-legged man with sandy hair and brows and a suit of severe black. His expression was ludicrously haughty. He gazed at the emerging innkeeper as if he were some particularly contemptible breed of insect. "Take me to Baron Ellerton's chamber at once," he commanded, in such ringing tones that Georgina heard him perfectly. Nonplussed, she hurried out to the corridor to intercept him.

"Here's the lady," said the innkeeper with patent relief when he saw her.

The newcomer turned and looked Georgina up and down. He was not precisely insolent, but she felt that he gauged the cut of her gown and elegance of her coif to a nicety. "Miss Georgina Goring?" he inquired.

"Yes?"

"I am Basil Jenkins, Baron Ellerton's man. I have come to take him home."

It took Georgina a moment to realize that this was the baron's valet. She had had no experience with the superior gentleman's gentleman, and thus was unprepared for his manner. But she recovered quickly. "He is far too unwell to travel," she answered. "The doctor scolded them even for bringing him the short distance to this inn."

"Indeed? Perhaps I could see for myself?" The man's tone suggested that he put little faith in the judgment of hysterical females, but Georgina found this amusing rather than offensive, particularly as she knew she was right. With a gesture, she invited him to follow her upstairs. And she did not speak again until Jenkins had seen the baron and returned to the hall outside his room.

"You see?" she asked then.

He nodded, his imperturbable facade gone. Seeing his genuine concern, Georgina added, "I hope you will stay and help me nurse him. My maid will also do what she can."

The valet drew himself up. "I shall do whatever is necessary, miss. You were very right to send for me, but there is no need for you to remain."

"You cannot sit with him every minute," retorted Georgina, stung. "You must sleep sometime."

"I'm sure the landlady will—"

"I intend to stay," she said flatly. "I have some experience as a nurse, and I mean to use it."

Jenkins eyed her with a mixture of suspicion and

annoyance. "And just what do you have to do with it, if you'll pardon my asking, miss? I don't recall hearing your name before you were so kind as to write."

Georgina stiffened, feeling herself on weak ground. "I am a friend of the baron's," she said.

"Are you now?" His gaze grew speculative, and Georgina nearly quailed under it.

But her instinctive dignity came to her aid. "I am," she replied coolly. "And I don't intend to discuss this matter further. You will want to see about a room for yourself and have your things brought up."

"The baron's things," he corrected.

She inclined her head majestically and swept past him and into Ellerton's room once again. But even as she heard him move away outside, her heart sank. It was clearly to be a battle for control of the sickroom, and she hated such brangles above all things.

10

From this point on, nothing went as Georgina had expected. She had unconsciously had a vision of herself moving efficiently around a darkened sickroom ministering to Ellerton, and perhaps later talking with him and amusing him through a boring time of recovery. Instead, wherever she turned, there was Jenkins, bringing a fresh jug of barley water, smoothing clean towels with complacent skill, unpacking the baron's things, or applying a cool cloth to his brow, his own innovation. Georgina felt useless, and increasingly annoyed. She suspected that Mr. Jenkins knew this, and enjoyed it, which made the situation worse. By the end of the first afternoon, she saw that she would have to make some stand or lose control entirely. Steeling herself, she poured out a cup of barley water and began to coax Ellerton to drink a little. Though he remained unconscious, he had once or twice been induced to drink.

"He won't take anything," whispered Jenkins from the corner where he was laying out Ellerton's toilet articles. "I tried him a moment since."

Georgina stayed where she was. "The doctor left orders that *I* should keep up the effort," she answered with a slight but unmistakable emphasis on the pronoun.

"Before *I* arrived," conceded Jenkins.

Georgina, having no success, straightened and put the cup aside. "Indeed. I am only glad I was on hand when the baron had no one else."

"Very fortunate," said the valet, with something very close to a sneer. "Though hardly necessary any longer, now that his *proper* attendants have arrived." Two more of the baron's servants had come in the late afternoon, to aid Jenkins, now that it was apparent Ellerton could not be taken home.

"Properly," replied Georgina, who was by this time more irritated than she could recall being in the course of an even-tempered life, "he should be nursed by the females of his family. It is too bad there are none, for such a task really *requires* a woman's special talents."

Jenkins drew his small frame up rigid. He was obviously put out both by her opposition and the fact that he had no ready riposte to this remark. But a muffled sound from the bed caused them to drop their argument and turn.

Ellerton's eyes were open, and he was watching them. As Jenkins hurried closer and Georgina bent to speak, he muttered, "Good God," and let his eyelids droop.

"Baron Ellerton," said Georgina. "How do you feel?"

"Let him be," objected the valet. "He needs his rest."

"The doctor said he could not tell his condition until he woke," snapped Georgina.

"I kept dreaming of that fiendish cat," murmured Ellerton in a thready voice. "Is my leg broken?"

"Yes," said Georgina.

"Umm. And ribs, I think." He moved very slightly, and grimaced. "What of the horses, and the phaeton?"

Georgina, who had not inquired deeply into their fate, was forced to draw back, chagrined.

"The team will be all right, Hotchkiss says," volunteered Jenkins eagerly. "They were pretty thoroughly blown, but he's taken them back to London and is looking after them. The phaeton's broken a wheel and axle and the paint's spoiled."

Ellerton nodded, as if this was no more than he expected, and closed his eyes again. But after a moment they snapped open to focus on Georgina. "Miss Wyndham?"

"She's all right. She wasn't hurt."

"Ah. Unsurprising. What are you doing here?"

"Just what I was asking before you woke, my lord," blurted Jenkins. "Now that I've come to look after you, I'm sure there's no need for the young lady to remain."

"Susan sent for me," answered Georgina, her gaze steady on the baron.

Jenkins' glance grew sharp. "I thought you told me you were traveling and happened upon his lordship here?"

Ellerton took in the situation at once. "Very kind of you," he said in a stronger voice. "I'm grateful."

The valet looked from one to the other. "But she needn't stay now, eh, my lord?" he repeated.

Starting to agree, his master met Georgina's clear gray eyes once again. In his weakness, he felt a strong desire for her company. "She *need* not, of course. She has done far too much already. But I admit I should be glad if she stayed."

Jenkins was dumbfounded. Georgina smiled. "I should be happy to do what I can," she murmured.

Ellerton smiled fleetingly as well; then his meager strength gave out and he drifted into a light slumber.

After this, there was nothing more Jenkins could say. Through the doctor's call (and profuse apologies for its lateness), Mason's more optimistic assessment, and preparations for dinner, he was generally silent, merely muttering to himself from time to time and venting his feelings through sharp commands to his fellow servants. Georgina had to smile more than once, but she was careful to hide her reaction, knowing that it would only make things worse. She had nearly concluded that the valet was vanquished when, as they sat together in the sickroom later that evening, he said, "My lord's accident will break a deal of hearts in London." He spoke absently, as if to himself, but his words were perfectly audible to Georgina. "He's popular with the ladies, he is," Jenkins continued. "And no wonder, I always say. But it's amazing the lengths they'll go to to put themselves in his way. Why, I recall one—a countess she was, and so lovely it made your eyes ache—pretended she'd hurt her ankle outside our front door. Had herself carried in to the drawing-room sofa, and stayed the whole afternoon. His lordship wasn't fooled, of course." He paused reminiscently. "And then there was the young lady from the country who claimed she was a cousin. Called his lordship 'dear cousin' so often I thought he would break. But he's always polite, my lord is. Never speaks ill of a lady, or to her, though he manages to thwart all their little schemes anyhow. A downy one, and no mistake."

He paused, and Georgina knew that he was glancing sidewise to see what effect his remarks had had on her. Her cheeks were flushed. She couldn't help that, for it had been only too clear that he was classifying her with these women who ran after the baron. But she sat straight, her chin high, and refused to give him the satisfaction of seeing that she was embarrassed. Ellerton could not believe this, or he would never had sanctioned her stay.

"No, his lordship's taste in women is somewhat different," continued Jenkins musingly. "His latest, now, she *is* a caution. All that black hair and those dark eyes. And a temper!" He chuckled as if recalling some incident. "I suppose it helps her on the stage."

Georgina grew even more rigid, and at the small movement she made, Jenkins clasped his hands together and pretended horror. "Miss! I beg your pardon. I quite forgot you were there. Talking to myself, I was, as I often do when I'm waiting up for his lordship. I'm not accustomed to having another person in his bedchamber, you know." He made this sound scandalous.

Georgina rose, routed. "I'm going to bed," was her only reply. "I will take your place first thing in the morning."

The valet had stood when she did. "I do hope you will forgive me, miss."

Georgina turned back to look at him, her understanding of his purpose clear in her eyes. To his credit, Jenkins quailed a little. Without answering, she went out.

But when she had put on her nightdress and gotten into bed, Georgina could not dismiss the man's tales from her mind. Indeed, they had conjured up, only too vividly, visions of the many young ladies who had pursued Ellerton, subtly and blatantly, and of the few he had granted his favor. The latter in particular preoccupied Georgina. She knew very little about such women, but Jenkins had painted a compelling portrait. Georgina's active imagination required no more to weave a series of scenes that greatly depressed her spirits.

More embarrassing was the valet's equation of her with the girls who had thrown themselves at Ellerton's feet, some literally. Jenkins clearly thought her another of these, and her wish to nurse the baron merely a scheme to capture his attention and stay by his side. Rehearsing his remarks made Georgina blush anew, for she saw that some would agree with him. Though it is completely untrue, Georgina thought fiercely. But some part of her remained uneasy.

Feeling that she must understand her motives completely if she were to face the days ahead, Georgina asked herself why she was determined to stay on at the inn. Jenkins was correct in arguing that he and the baron's other servants could care for him adequately. Was she acting as those other women had? Georgina wondered.

She was trying to help, she insisted, and to shield Susan from the possible consequences of her foolhardy behavior. But the annoying skeptical voice in her mind replied that her help was not necessary, and that she made Susan's position more precarious, rather than less so, by staying. While she was here, there was more likelihood that her family would be associated with Ellerton's accident. People who had seen Susan driving with him might recall it and make the connection. If Georgina went home, there would be no reason to associate them with the baron.

Yet as sensible as this seemed, Georgina resisted it. *She* would not wish to be left alone at an inn, injured and weak, with only servants, she told herself. And though Jenkins seemed very capable, he showed no signs of having nursed a sick man before, as Georgina had. Moreover, Ellerton's condition was Susan's fault, and it was only right that the family make some amends. Susan could not, so Georgina would. The only unfortunate thing was that she could not explain this to those who would undoubtedly find her presence startling.

Trying to feel virtuous at her adherence to duty, Georgina turned over for perhaps the twentieth time and ordered herself to sleep. She would be no good to anyone tomorrow if she did not. But a part of her remained unsatisfied, and each time she closed her eyes, a procession of women passed before her mind's eye—demure, laughing, boldly vivacious, and all beautiful and utterly self-assured. Nothing, thought Georgina despondently, like herself. Baron Ellerton could have no such interest in her. She recalled his remarks about her odd character.

"Then no one will link you with those women who pursued him," said Georgina aloud. "It will not occur to them!" And pulling the bedclothes up over her chin, she commanded herself to sleep.

It was apparent the following morning, with Georgina's maid settled in and all her things unpacked, that she had one advantage at least in the sickroom. She could establish herself in the armchair with her books and her sewing and easily hold the field, while Jenkins, who failed to depart with the coming of daylight, had to find reasons for his presence. The fifth time he adjusted the baron's pillows, eliciting an impatient sound from Ellerton, Georgina had to hide a smile. She understood some of the valet's feelings at finding a stranger in charge of his master, but she would not have been human had she not enjoyed her small triumph after last night.

At one, when Georgina went downstairs for luncheon, she was greeted by her four young friends, who had ridden out to visit her and inquire whether she needed anything. "How is he?" was the first remark, voiced by Marianne but obviously a general concern.

"A little better. He woke last night for a while, and has been awake most of this morning. The doctor thinks he will be all right, though very weak for a time."

Susan looked distinctly relieved.

"Have his servants arrived to help you?" asked William.

Georgina nodded, and her expression was so wry that Marianne inquired further. "It is his valet," replied Georgina. "He is . . . difficult."

No one but Marianne appeared to find this of interest, or comprehensible. The other three, assured of Ellerton's improvement, had turned their attention to ordering luncheon. "I understand that the personal attendants of men of fashion are often so," said Marianne quietly. "Their work requires such fussiness."

"I think he is simply jealous," responded Georgina.

"Ah. Not accustomed to interference in his arrangements." Marianne nodded.

The other was surprised, and grateful, at this ready comprehension. "Exactly. He wishes Baron Ellerton to rely on no one but himself, I think. He seems much attached to him."

"Perhaps he is a family retainer. I hope you are not finding things too unpleasant?"

"Oh no."

"You could, I suppose, leave them to his servants now." The look that passed over Georgina's face at this suggestion made her hurriedly add, "Though I'm sure Baron Ellerton would find that less pleasant."

"I think we owe him some return, after Susan's foolishness." Georgina's tone was unnatural, and she dropped her eyes.

"Of course." But Marianne eyed her with new concern. She had been pleased to find that Susan Wyndham had put aside all thoughts of Ellerton after their disastrous adventure. Indeed, she had laughed with the other girl this morning over the ridiculous idea of their rivalry for his attentions, a rivalry that had been wholly the creation of Susan's imagination. And they had agreed on the unlikelihood of the baron's being smitten with either of them, Susan because he now seemed much less appealing and Marianne from a more realistic perspective. The latter was discomfited to see signs of attraction in Georgina, whom she had thought so sensible and likable. Marianne's immediate impulse was to warn her, though she could see that this would not be welcome. She did not wish to let Georgina be hurt. Yet it was obvious that her advice was neither sought nor desired. And speaking might well prevent any future talk on the subject. Undecided, she kept silent.

"Georgina," said Susan then. "Do you want cold ham or cold beef? *I* want ham."

"But I thought we agreed," began Tony hotly.

"Why not have both?" offered Georgina.

The two young people seemed much struck.

Smiling, William Wyndham came over to join her. "We are in for a feast, I think. They are ordering whatever either of them wants."

"We'll make them pay, then," replied Marianne, and the two exchanged smiles.

"But what can we do for you in town, Georgina?" he continued. "That is why we came, after all."

"I have all I need just now. I will call on you when necessary."

"See that you do."

"How are things in London? Did Aunt Sybil and Lady Bentham take your news well?"

"Grandmama was agog," laughed William. "I believe she would be here now if there were any means of fitting her bed into a carriage. Do you think she has a *tendre* for Ellerton?"

Georgina's answering smile was stiff, and Marianne spoke before William could notice it. "Mama, on the other hand, scarcely heard what I said, I think. But she is happy to have Susan accompany us when we go out."

"Poor woman," said William. "She has no idea what she is taking on. But you may count on me to support you."

The look that William and Marianne exchanged then made Georgina frown thoughtfully.

"Are you coming to the table?" complained Tony. "I'm half-starved."

"You're always half-starved," William retorted, but he turned to usher the ladies to their chairs. "Anyone would think your parents never fed you."

"I'm an orphan," responded Tony with mournful dignity, "with no one in the world to watch over me." His hazel eyes sparkled with reproach.

"Except an immensely rich cousin who dotes on you, from all reports," laughed William, "and a worshipful older sister."

"Worshipful!" Tony appeared amazed and revolted. "Someday I shall present you to Amanda, and you will see just how worshipful she is. Why, her husband—"

"*I* am going to eat," declared Susan, picking up her fork. She had been seated for some time.

Abandoning his argument, Tony hastened to join her, and they were all soon engrossed in the landlord's fine cold meats and fruit. Georgina enjoyed herself surprisingly, and it was clear that the other four were having a splendid time. Indeed, sitting back to watch them for a moment in the midst of the meal, Georgina felt a pang of envy along with her pleasure in their happiness. They all seemed so carefree, their lively laughter unmarred by concerns more serious than which party they would attend that night. Yet when the time came for them to depart, and she returned to Ellerton's sickroom, her envy faded at once. Jenkins had at last gone to get some sleep, and Georgina and the baron talked quietly together at intervals. When Ellerton dozed, she read or sewed, and throughout the afternoon she was filled with a warm contentment.

11

The journey back to London was not entirely gay. In the first place, Susan and Tony could not seem to speak to one another without quarreling. They began on departure from the innyard, disputing the merits of Tony's mount, and continued through every foot of the ride, bickering over the chance of a shortcut, the probable hour of their arrival home, and a thousand other things. William and Marianne gradually fell back, putting enough distance between them so that they could hear only the constant rhythm of argument, not the specifics.

"They might be brother and sister," said Marianne with a smile.

"Susan never argued with *us*," corrected William. "She commanded, and we obeyed. Or didn't. And then there was a fearful row. But not like that." He nodded toward the two ahead. "They seem to be enjoying themselves."

Marianne agreed, impressed by his perspicacity. "That sounds like my brother. He was always commanding, too, though I seldom listened." She smiled again. "At least until he married Alicia."

William smiled back at her. "And then you listened?" he teased.

"Then he stopped being so silly." They laughed together.

"So you don't care for commands?" he added.

"Not much."

William watched her profile as they rode along the grassy lane Susan and Tony had insisted was a quicker way back to London. Marianne looked resplendent with the sun lighting her red hair to molten copper where it curled from beneath her hat and the lines of her body clear in her deep blue riding habit. William had never met a girl who attracted him more. He wanted at the same time to learn everything about her, and to throw caution to the winds and sweep her into his arms.

Marianne felt his gaze, but did not turn at first. Her own feelings were less certain than William's. She knew she liked him, and she was intrigued by his air of maturity and command. In London, to which her experience of the male sex was generally limited, men seemed either callow and stammering or arrogantly self-assured. Marianne had thought until Lord Robert Devere offered for her that she favored the latter, who most resembled her beloved brother, but now she wasn't sure. And William was a third sort of man. He had assurance without a trace of arrogance. She turned her head and met his admiring look. Their eyes were nearly the same color, she realized.

Their gaze held for a moment that seemed to stretch far longer. Wordlessly they communicated their special interest in one another, each thrilling to the knowledge that the feeling was mutual. Their surroundings receded into a humming blur.

"William!" called Susan urgently from just ahead. "Hurry. There's a storm coming."

Both William and Marianne started visibly and

turned to her. Susan and Tony had pulled up and were much closer than before, though they did not appear to have noticed anything unusual. Susan was motioning them forward emphatically. "Come on!"

Glancing upward, they saw at once that she was correct. As they talked, a line of dark clouds had raced in from the east, and a heavy shower was imminent. When Susan saw that they understood, she immediately turned her horse and kicked it into a gallop, hoping to outrun the rain. Tony was hot on her heels.

"They won't make it," judged William.

Marianne was looking around, but found no shelter. "No."

"And they led us into this cursed lane where there are no houses at all."

She nodded, then abruptly laughed. "I'll race you." And before he could reply, she was off.

William lost a valuable moment looking after her. Then he recovered and set his heels to his mount.

The four of them thundered down the empty lane, Susan and Tony well to the front, Marianne next, and William gaining on her. Susan's laughter floated back over the grass, and when Marianne glanced over her shoulder, she was grinning.

A bolt of lightning made them urge their horses on, and the animals needed no further encouragement when thunder followed. But their speed was in the end to no avail, for they had not reached the end of the lane when the skies opened. A torrent poured down upon them, soaking all four in the first minute. The rain fell straight down, so heavily that it seemed there was no space between drops, and it was difficult to see more than a few feet ahead. Shocked by the sudden onslaught, Marianne slowed her horse to a walk, and William soon drew up alongside. Susan and Tony, invisible in the storm, apparently continued to gallop, for their excited whoops gradually faded with distance.

Marianne breathed in gasps. The rain pounded at them, and it had started so abruptly that she was still breathless with the shock. She glanced at William; huge raindrops were striking the top of his head so violently that they sent up tiny circles of spray, and water was pouring down his face so that he had to keep blinking and sputtering. She tipped her head a little more forward to better take advantage of her hat brim and to hide a giggle. "Where is your hat?"

"What?" The roar of the storm kept him from hearing.

"Your hat!"

"Oh. Gone. This confounded rain knocked it into the ditch, and I decided it wasn't worth getting down." He stopped, coughing, then added, "We've got to get out of this."

Marianne merely nodded. She found it difficult to converse at a shout.

William kicked his mount to a reluctant trot, and they moved forward more rapidly again. Susan and Tony had disappeared.

It was nearly impossible to see anything in the heavy downpour. Indeed, at moments they feared to stray off the ill-marked lane. But occasionally the rain seemed to part like a curtain and afford glimpses of the country. In one of these, Marianne saw something. "Look there!" she shouted, pointing. But by the time William had turned, the view was obscured again. "I saw a building," insisted the girl. "Off that way, perhaps twenty yards."

"Are you sure?" cried William.

At Marianne's decisive nod, he turned his horse's head to follow hers. She negotiated the shallow ditch at the side of the road and began to push through the bushes beyond. At any other time she would have avoided the dripping vegetation, but she could not get any wetter. Almost at once, they came to a narrow path, just wide enough for a farm cart, and in a short time reached a small dilapidated barn at the edge of a field.

William jumped down and tried the door, which, mercifully, was unlatched. He pushed it wide, and Marianne rode in, William leading his mount just behind. Inside, it was musty but dry. Marianne slid from her saddle and gave a great sigh of relief. It was wonderful to be out of the rain. Standing beneath a roof, listening to it pounding above, filled her with an exquisite feeling of coziness, despite her soaked garments.

William led their horses to the far corner of the barn, where a few wisps of hay tempted them. "No use rubbing them down," he concluded. "We'll be going on soon."

Marianne unpinned her hat and pulled it off, a spray of droplets fanning out from the feather that had once adorned it and now drooped soddenly along the brim. She shook her head, and her red hair escaped its binding and fanned out across her shoulders, part drenched and part dry where it had been protected by the bonnet.

William had to stifle a gasp. With her radiant hair all down around her face, Marianne was more beautiful than ever.

Unaware of his reaction, she put the hat down and bent to try to wring the water from her skirt. The long sweep of a riding habit was always cumbersome on the ground, but wet, it was impossibly weighty. "We should shut the door, don't you think?" she said without looking up. "It is begining to blow in."

As if physically prodded, William sprang toward the door and closed it, then turned to stare at Marianne again. He could not help it.

"Water is dripping off your coat tails," she said, laughing a little as she pointed at them. "You should try wringing, though I am not having much luck." When he didn't move, she raised her eyes to his face, and what she saw there stifled speech. Marianne was suddenly conscious of the way her wet habit molded to every curve of her body, and of her hair in wild disarray about her face. She flushed vividly and abandoned her efforts to dry her skirt. Its water-logged folds dragging over the dirt floor, she moved to the horses, hiding her scarlet face by turning her back. "How are you, Willow?" she asked her mount. She put a hand on the mare's shoulder, and it twitched. "It's all right," she murmured.

Under control again, Marianne turned. "We can't keep them here long; they'll take cold."

William, too, had sternly repressed his emotions. "And we shall contract a desperate chill." He went to look through the narrow opening he had left in the door. "It is letting up a bit, I think." But he didn't sound convinced.

"It can't go on raining this heavily for long," responded Marianne. "And perhaps Susan and Tony will discover a carriage and come back for us."

William nodded, trying to look optimistic. But his knowledge of Susan suggested it was far more likely she would settle herself in some comfortable shelter and wait for them to arrive. The proprieties of the situation would never occur to her, he thought bitterly.

An awkward silence fell, the first in the history of their acquaintance. Before, it had seemed they always had something to say to one another; now, suddenly, they had nothing. Every remark that Marianne thought of, and prepared to voice, seemed unwise or inane. She wanted to speak, to show William that she was perfectly at ease and thought nothing of the necessity of their remaining together here for some time—indeed, that she was quite pleased to do so—but the English language seemed inexplicably full of pitfalls, when a few minutes before it had been innocuous.

William scarcely noticed her silence, however. He was wrestling with far more compelling problems. He had nearly pulled her into his arms, he thought guiltily, and he could not wholly repress the desire to do so even now. It was despicable. Marianne was under his care and in his power; he could not take advantage of this accident to force himself upon her. The mere idea made him furious. Yet whenever he looked at her . . . He savagely cut off this line of thought. "Perhaps we should just ride on," he said, his tone so harsh that Marianne blinked. "We cannot get any wetter, after all, and it may go on raining for hours."

"You don't think—?"

"I have said what I think!"

She stiffened, offended at his peremptory accents and unable to see what was causing this sudden unpleasantness. "I should prefer to wait awhile," she answered coldly.

Irrationally, William felt as if this made everything her fault. Could she not see the difficulty? he wondered angrily. "It is . . . unsuitable," he replied.

At this, and recalling the look in his eyes a few

moments before, Marianne did see. She flushed slightly again, at the same time amazed at herself. She was behaving quite uncharacteristically, she thought. She was no simpering milk-and-water miss, afraid to be left alone with a man for an instant; she never had been. What was it about Sir William Wyndham. . .? She raised her eyes and met his, dropping them again at once. "Perhaps you're right," she said shakily.

William, inexplicably, felt disappointed. But he strode at once to the horses and turned them toward the door. After quickly checking the harness, he looked at Marianne.

"You'll have to throw me up," she added in a voice that she scarcely recognized as her own. "There's no block, and my skirts . . ." She gestured helplessly.

"Of course." William might have been speaking to a stranger, one he did not find particularly amiable. His cool courtesy was immensely discouraging. Standing beside her mare, he laced his fingers together and bent to allow her to step into them, his eyes resolutely on the floor.

Marianne put a hand on his shoulder and slowly raised her boot. For some reason, she felt rather like crying. William grasped her foot and prepared to throw her into the saddle as the girl tensed for the jump.

In the next instant, they both moved, but Marianne's riding boot was slicked with mud from its soaking and subsequent movement about the dirt floor, and the floor itself was slippery with the water they and their animals had brought in. William slipped, and Marianne's foot slid in his hands, and the two went down in a confused heap together, entangled in her heavy skirts.

"I . . . I *beg* your pardon," gasped William, struggling to sit up and finding himself trapped by sodden cloth. He pushed out with his arms, and discovered to his horror that they were entwined around Marianne's waist.

"It wasn't your fault," she responded, and twisted to kick her feet free of the folds of her dress. This brought her face to face with William, hardly two inches away, and made her vividly aware of his arms about her and the feel of his body along the length of hers. He was very warm against the chill of her wet clothes. "It was slippery," she added on a gasp.

Their eyes locked, and all thoughts of propriety went out of William's mind. He knew only that he held this lovely girl close, as he had longed to do, and that she did not seem revolted. Indeed, her look held tremulous signs of encouragement. Without thinking further, he bent his head and fastened his lips on hers. Marianne, equally rapt, wound her arms about his neck.

The kiss seemed to go on forever. They forgot that they were lying on a muddied dirt floor; they forgot the rain and their companions; indeed, they forgot all the world except each other. Each had kissed before, William rather more than Marianne, but neither had experienced anything like the passion that ran through them now. It seemed to Marianne as if the two of them merged into one creature, with one mind and one desire.

Then, slowly, reluctantly, the kiss ended. They drew a little apart, both breathing fast, and gazed at one another again. For a long moment, their looks were rapturous. Then William stiffened and began to struggle upright again. "I'm sorry," he choked out. "I shouldn't have . . . I didn't mean . . ." He finally got free of the habit and stood, holding out a hand to help her up.

"You didn't mean to kiss me?" inquired Marianne, who was much less flustered now than earlier.

"No!"

"Strange. You seemed to mean it." She knew what he was feeling, but she couldn't resist teasing him. To Marianne, it seemed that all had been settled between them in that kiss. There were a number of wearisome details remaining, of course, chiefly his offer and her acceptance, but each of them knew the outcome. The only important thing was what had just passed between them.

William, however, was feeling far different. He was, in the first place, raging with self-blame for giving in to the impulses he had been fighting so hard. Whatever his intentions toward Marianne, he told himself, he had behaved abominably. But of more concern was the next step. William wanted nothing more than to ask Marianne to be his wife and to resume, with such sanction, their previous activity. But he was acutely aware of certain impediments.

Marianne MacClain—*Lady* Marianne, he corrected himself miserably—was the daughter and sister of an earl. Though the Wyndhams were a fine old family, they had never risen above a knighthood, and their fortune was merely comfortable, while Marianne's was munificent. She could make a far more brilliant match than he. Moreover, and worse, William knew quite well that she had refused a man last Season who had had all the things he did not. What would she think when he proposed marriage? She might well laugh in his face. Or slap it, which was what he deserved after today. That Marianne had responded eagerly to his advances, and that she was smiling expectantly at him now, William was too miserable to acknowledge. He could think only that he loved this girl with all his heart and could not have her. "I . . . I cannot apologize sufficiently for my unforgivable behavior," he stammered at last. "Perhaps it would be best if we simply rode on, and put it from our minds. I swear to you I will never do such a thing again."

Marianne gaped at him, astonished and feeling the beginnings of bitter disappointment.

He misinterpreted her look. "I know it seems impossible to go on as if nothing had happened," he said. "But I do not see any alternative. I will, of course, keep out of your way after this."

"You . . . you . . ." Marianne could not think of an epithet harsh enough. She could not believe that he was rejecting her.

"You cannot hate me more than I do myself," replied William unhappily. "Come, let us go." He offered his laced fingers again, and Marianne was too hurt and angry to do anything but acquiesce. This time, she mounted without mishap, and William followed suit at once. He pushed open the door and waited for her to ride through. The rain was somewhat less, merely a heavy shower now, and the water served to wash the mud from their clothes. They rode in silence to the lane and turned along it. They had not gone far before they met Susan and Tony coming back.

"Where have you *been?*" exclaimed Susan through the rain. "Tony insisted we come back for you. What took you so long? We might have found shelter by now and been out of this awful rain, if you had only kept up."

"Sorry," replied William gruffly, and he spurred his horse ahead.

"Anything the matter?" wondered Tony, sensing the tension.

"Nothing whatever," snapped Marianne. "Can we go on now? I am soaked to the skin." And she followed William, at a distance, in his gallop.

Susan and Tony exchanged a bewildered look. "Well, why didn't they keep up, if they are in such a hurry?" asked Susan, and they turned their mounts to follow.

12

Several days passed without incident at the posting house. Ellerton regained strength slowly and was not capable at first of long conversations or sustained attention. Georgina established a quiet routine, sitting in the sickroom reading or sewing in the morning and afternoon, taking her meals in a private parlor downstairs, and sometimes walking near the inn for fresh air and exercise. After the second day, Jenkins was forced to sleep most of the day, as Georgina had predicted. Not even his devotion could erase the need for rest in the intervals of his night watches. Thus Georgina's days grew easier, and she once again felt truly useful to the baron. Though Jenkins would sooner have cut out his tongue than acknowledge her contribution, and though he slept as little as possible and hung about Ellerton's chamber, he told no more anecdotes about the baron's female admirers, and even, at the end of the week, admitted to the doctor that Miss Goring was a fair nurse. When Dr. Mason repeated this to her, Georgina had to smile, for she knew that Jenkins would be mortified if he found out she had been told. But her early antipathy to the man was giving way to amusement as they adjusted to each other, and Jenkins' unquestionable loyalty and unflagging industry in caring for his master impressed her; she had no intention of taxing him with his compliment.

A week and a half after the accident, Ellerton showed definite signs of improvement. He slept far less, ate more, and began to complain of boredom. At this point, Georgina's task became far harder than Jenkins', for Ellerton remained awake the whole day and rested peacefully most of the night. After one afternoon of complaints, she even considered asking the valet to change with her, but she could not bring herself to admit defeat, and when her annoyance faded she admitted that she didn't really wish it.

On Tuesday morning, when Georgina came into the room, the valet met her near the door. "He woke very early today, miss," he told her. "And a bit irritable."

Since Jenkins had never before voiced even so mild a criticism of his employer, Georgina prepared herself for a difficult day. The valet looked very tired, she noticed; his eyes were reddened, and his face haggard. "You should get a good long sleep," she whispered sympathetically.

This instantly brought back his suspicions. "I can look after myself, thank you, miss." And with a little bow, he went out.

Georgina shook her head and went to her armchair. Ellerton appeared to be drowsing, so she picked up her book from the table and opened it. But instead of reading, she found herself gazing at the far wall and musing over her situation. It really was ridiculous, she thought, the way she and Jenkins vied with each other for supremacy. There was no reason they should be rivals, for they both wanted the same thing. At the idea of rivalry, Georgina's lips curved upward.

First Susan and Marianne had thought themselves rivals for the baron's affections, or Susan had seen it so, at least, and now she and Jenkins were being equally silly, though she claimed for herself Marianne's part. The contest was of Jenkins' creation. Amused, Georgina developed the comparison in her mind until finally the ludicrousness of it struck her so forcibly that she laughed aloud, at once stifling the sound and glancing at Ellerton to see that she had not disturbed him.

The baron was wide-awake, and watching her with an interested gaze. "What is the joke?" he asked, as if they were in the midst of a conversation.

Georgina flushed slightly. "I was only thinking of something."

"Obviously." He waited for her to tell him what.

She did not feel she could. It would mean exposing Susan and Marianne, and herself. "A private matter," she replied, and before he could object, added, "Have you had your breakfast?"

"Yes, I have. And I have been shaved and combed and fussed over until I am half-mad. And now I shall lie here in bed all day with nothing to do. I am abandoned wholly without amusement, and now you refuse to so much as share a joke." He tried to look piteous.

Georgina hid a smile. He sounded much more like a small boy than an elegant Corinthian. "You have had a number of visitors."

"Cruel, Miss Goring! Do you not know that there is nothing more infuriating than laughing aloud, then keeping the reason to yourself? It is nearly as bad as assuring one you have a secret which you can on no account tell, perhaps worse."

"I begin to better understand the old saying about

idle hands," responded Georgina. "They might better say idle minds give rise to mischief. I don't believe you care a whit for the joke; you are merely lightening your boredom by rallying me."

"Miss Goring!" But though he pretended shock, an arrested look in his blue eyes showed that she had scored a hit. "I am thinking of nothing but this joke, I promise you. I daresay I shan't be able to put it from my mind. I shall become obsessed and develop brain fever, I suppose."

"You are feeling better, aren't you?" commented Georgina. She had not seen him so lively since the accident.

"On the contrary, I am worse. I begin to find this room and this bed intolerable. I shall ask the doctor for a pair of crutches today and get out a bit."

"But he said you mustn't move for two weeks, at least," replied Georgina, alarmed.

"He doesn't know my iron constitution." Ellerton smiled a little. "You needn't look so worried, Miss Goring. I said I meant to ask the doctor, and I shall abide by his decision. I fancy he was being overcautious."

Georgina nodded, realizing that her concern was exaggerated by her own reluctance to end this interlude just as he was improving and able to talk. This was inexcusably selfish, she scolded silently.

"And so, what about the joke?" he continued when she did not speak.

"Do you never give up?"

"Never!"

"Even though I have told you it was a private matter?"

"That is what one always says to silence awkward questions. Is it really true in this case?"

"Yes!"

"Ah. Well, then, I mustn't inquire further."

His expression was so comical that Georgina burst out laughing. "I have never met a man so curious, or so determined in his curiosity. I was thinking about Jenkins." She stopped, sorry to have revealed this much.

"It is true," he replied judiciously. "Curiosity has always been my besetting sin. It often gets me into trouble, but on the other hand, I have learned a great many useful things." He paused. "Jenkins, now. I should be happy to know something amusing about him. He is usually such a solemn fellow. Some mornings, when he comes in with my coffee, I am quite cast down by his portentous manner."

Georgina laughed again. "It is really nothing. You make me ashamed to tell it. I was merely thinking of Jenkins' jealousy over the nursing. He so hates to let anyone help."

"Ah. Yes, he is rather like a mother hen."

This comparison was so apt that Georgina had to laugh again. She felt a bit guilty to be mocking Jenkins in this way, but Ellerton had insisted, and she had seen no other way to shelter Susan except by sacrificing the valet.

"You and he are not dreadfully at odds, I hope?" added the baron.

"Oh, no. We have reached a truce."

His eyes gleamed appreciatively, and Georgina was certain that he understood more than she had said. "What do you think of him?"

"Mr. Jenkins?" She was surprised.

"The same."

"Well, I . . . Nothing, really. He seems a very good servant, and he is devoted to you."

"Come, come, you expressed a much more natural opinion a few moments ago. What do you think of him as a specimen of human nature?"

This reminded Georgina of a conversation they had had some time ago. "I am not in the habit of considering people as 'specimens,' Baron Ellerton."

"No? I'm not so sure. I think you are as avid a student of the subject as I." She started to object, but he forestalled her. "Watching your face as you thought of your 'joke,' I distinctly observed some of the same delight in oddity. I am convinced you share my interest in unusual situations and personalities. That is one reason I insisted upon hearing it. As well as my insatiable curiosity, of course."

"I don't think of my friends and acquaintances as 'oddities,' " answered Georgina stiffly, recalling more of that talk and his characterization of her.

"Of course you do not. Why so haughty? There is nothing ill-natured or wrong in what I say. Indeed, it was just such an impulse that allowed us to make one another's acquaintance in the beginning."

When he had rescued Susan and Marianne, at the first ball, thought Georgina. He was interested only in her "oddity." The thought hurt surprisingly.

"Why else are you here, after all?" he finished, and his words so echoed Georgina's thought that she gaped. "Come, come, do you claim that you were not taken with the unusual, and ridiculous, elements of this situation? *I* certainly would have been, had I not been knocked unconsious. A mere chit, who looks as if she could not stand in a high wind, succeeds in usurping my phaeton, wrecking it, and consigning me to a sickbed, and comes away without a scratch. And then I, who have some little reputation both as a whip and as a man of the world, am left to be rescued by this girl and her friends. If I were not the victim, I should call that the most amusing story I have heard in years."

Georgina had to laugh.

"There, you see? How is your charming cousin, by the by?"

"Very well."

"I had no doubt of it. Enjoying the Season, I suppose?"

She nodded, trying not to laugh again.

"Having forgotten all about her little contretemps with my phaeton."

"Of course she has not forgotten! Susan is . . ." Georgina hesitated, remembered her cousin's rapid dismissal of her mistake.

"Precisely," said the baron, as if making the final, conclusive point in an argument.

"We have done everything possible to give her a proper sense of her, er, overexuberance," answered Georgina stiffly.

"A fine word for mayhem and near-murder," he responded admiringly. "What will you call it when she does manage to kill someone, I wonder. By the by, I hope *I* succeeded in ridding the world of that hellish cat?"

Georgina was sternly forbidding herself to laugh again. "Daisy? No, he's fine. He found his way home all alone."

He was staring incredulously. "Daisy? I am referring to a very large ginger-colored animal with the character of a Tothill Fields assassin."

Georgina nodded, her laughter escaping.

"Its *name* is . . . No, you needn't tell me. Miss Wyndham christened it, of course."

"She was very young," gasped Georgina.

"That girl was never young," declared the baron, his eyes twinkling.

"I . . . I shouldn't laugh." She strove for control.

"Why not? Does this strike you as cruelty?"

This brought her up short. "No," she replied after a moment. "But it is . . ."

"Yes?" He looked politely interested.

"Well, if Susan were here . . ."

"I should speak just as I have, and no doubt a lively discussion would ensue."

"Lively, indeed!"

"I am fascinated by human nature, not contemptuous of it, Miss Goring. And I pride myself on understanding its foibles."

This gave Georgina much to ponder, for it was true that she felt an answering impulse in herself when he spoke of his "study." She had resisted her own bent in this direction, feeling it was a sign of false superiority, but now she began to wonder. Unfortunately, Dr. Mason called just then, and the conversation was dropped. It remained vivid in Georgina's mind, however.

Ellerton was refused crutches, but the doctor did say he might be carried to a sofa downstairs for part of the day, and he seemed satisfied with this concession. In the afternoon, it was accordingly done, and a party of visitors arrived soon after to inquire about him. Georgina, as was her custom on such occasions, retreated to her own room. She had no wish to be found sitting at Ellerton's side by members of the *haut ton*. It was enough that she was vaguely known to be helping with the nursing. And the baron was unlikely to need her now.

She was just about to put on her hat and go out

for a short walk when there was a tap on her door. Opening it, she found Lady Marianne MacClain in the corridor, hands clasped around her riding crop. "How do you do?" said Georgina warmly. "I have not seen you for several days. Are the others here as well?"

"No, I rode out alone."

Georgina was a little surprised at this. When William and the others had come the last time, Marianne had not accompanied them. And though she had thought nothing about it at the time, this solitary visit made it appear more significant. Looking closer, she thought Marianne showed strain. But she said only, "I was just going walking. Would you care to come, or shall we remain here?"

"A walk would be nice," answered Marianne.

"Oh, but you are wearing riding dress, of course. You will not wish to—"

"It's quite all right," interrupted the other, more sharply than Georgina had ever heard her speak. She looped the trailing folds of her habit over her arm and turned toward the stairs.

Georgina said no more until they were outside the inn and strolling along the grassy lane that wandered out behind it, leading, as she had previously discovered, to a small village about a half-mile away. Then she ventured, "A fine day."

Marianne merely nodded.

"You did not come completely alone, I hope?"

"I brought my groom."

Having established to her own satisfaction that something was wrong with Marianne, Georgina fell silent, thinking how to approach the subject. They were not very well acquainted, but Marianne had come a good distance to see her, and that argued some sort of appeal. Georgina wished to help if she could. "The baron is much better," she offered. "He is allowed to lie on the sofa downstairs, and he has callers today."

"Ah," was the only reply.

Not Ellerton, then, concluded Georgina, conscious of a feeling of relief. "How is Tony? When I saw him last he had just purchased the most astonishing waistcoat."

Marianne smiled a little. "He has another, even more brilliant."

"No, how could it be? I had to shade my eyes against the last." They laughed together, and then Georgina suddenly realized why she must have come. "Susan has not fallen into another scrape, has she? I feel I am imposing dreadfully on your good nature in asking you to take her about, but—"

"No, no, Susan is very well. She is enjoying the Season hugely and has done nothing wrong."

Her tone implied that others were not experiencing such enjoyment, and Georgina glanced sideways at her, trying to discover the reason. "I suppose William is watching over her," she said, simply to fill the silence.

"Undoubtedly!" snapped Marianne, both bitter and derisive. "He should be very good at that."

"What is it?" asked Georgina, unable to ignore her tone. "Have you quarreled with William?"

To her complete astonishment, Marianne burst into tears.

At once Georgina was all efficiency. She took the other girl's arm and hurried her toward a spot she had found some days previously. It was a grassy nook amidst a grove of beeches near the road, invisible to the casual passerby and pleasantly warmed by the sun. Once there, she urged Marianne to sit on a fallen log and settled beside her, her arm remaining about the younger girl's shoulders. Gradually her tears abated, and when she began to search for a handkerchief, Georgina was ready with her own.

"I beg your pardon," said Marianne tremulously when she had blown her nose. "I did not mean to cry."

"It doesn't matter in the least," replied Georgina. "But what's the matter? *Is* it William?"

Marianne gazed at the grass, sprigged now with tiny pink and blue flowers. "I came to see you because I could think of no one else, but I don't believe I can tell you after all."

Georgina watched her face, perplexed. "You needn't tell me anything you don't wish to, of course, but I shall keep your confidence. And I should be happy to help, if I can."

"Oh, no one can *help*," responded Marianne.

Silence fell between them. Georgina wondered what she should say. Marianne began to cut off the grass tops with her riding crop.

"I must speak to someone!" blurted the latter finally. "Mama does not listen properly, and Ian and Alicia will not be home for months. I thought of Lady Goring, but I am not at all acquainted with her, and besides, if I called I might see . . . him. But I am so miserable, and I don't know what to do!"

"Tell me," commanded Georgina. "No one else shall hear of it." Her sympathy blotted out any awkwardness she might otherwise have felt at advising this polished young woman.

Haltingly Marianne began the story of her encounter with William during the storm. As she talked, the words seemed to flow more easily, and by the end she was speaking in a breathless rush. "So I suppose he thinks me some sort of horrid *fast* creature," she finished. "But I have never done such a thing before, Georgina. Never! Ian used to scold me about wishing to . . . oh, go to a masquerade, or dance too often with the same partner, but with William—Sir William, I mean—I was just . . . I can't explain it to you. I love him!"

This last rose to an anguished cry, and it was obvious to Georgina that Marianne had been accusing herself and indulging in agonies of remorse since the day this had happened. It was equally clear that her brother's early strictures had made her very sensitive on such matters, and less able to justify her actions than most. Georgina was amazed to discover that the girl she had thought so self-possessed and at ease was prey to these doubts. And she was delighted to know that she *could* be of help. She had known William most of his life, and she felt confident in interpreting his actions. She had noticed his interest in Marianne long ago, and its development into something deeper. The story she had been told confirmed her convictions, for William was not the sort of man to give way to his impulses unless they were very strong and acceptable to his highly developed code of honor. He loved Marianne, Georgina was certain.

"William is an admirable character in many ways," Georgina began. "He has a strong sense of responsibility, for example. I have always thought Susan had something to do with that." She smiled, though Marianne did not respond. "He is kind and loving and almost wholly without conceit. Unfortunately, the latter trait sometimes causes him to underrate his own abilities or attractions, and to fail to get what he wants because of diffidence in asking for it."

Marianne's woeful expression began to shift, and her blue eyes sharpened.

"I have seen it happen more than once," Georgina continued, "even over quite important things, though none this important, of course."

"Do you mean . . . ?" began Marianne, and stopped.

"William loves you as much as you do him, but I imagine he can't quite bring himself to say so. I know he would blame himself for the incident you described, berating himself for taking advantage of you."

"Any man with sense could have seen that I—"

"Ah, but in this area, William's usual good sense deserts him, the more so as he becomes more serious. And you must remember, Marianne, that there are differences in your rank and fortune—"

"Who cares for those?" she interrupted impatiently.

"William," responded Georgina. "And he would also remember your reputation."

"My . . . ?" Marianne's eyes clouded with doubt again.

"As the girl who refused the most brilliant match the *ton* had to offer," finished Georgina, teasing a little.

Her face cleared. "But that was entirely different. Lord Devere was . . . I did not love him!"

"William would not be sure of the difference."

"What idiots men are!" But her misery had dissipated.

"They do seem very dull at times," agreed Georgina.

"But what am I to do? I utterly refuse to propose to *him*!"

Georgina smiled. "Indeed, you should not. Shall I speak to him?"

"You mean, tell him to offer for me? No!"

"I believe I could be a bit more subtle than—"

"If he cannot muster the courage to ask me himself, then let him go."

"But don't you think—"

"No." Marianne jumped up, all her confidence and vitality seemingly restored by Georgina's assurances. "I have no patience with him if that is what he thinks. He ought to be able to *see* how I feel."

"Well . . . but, Marianne—"

"Promise you won't say anything."

"I have promised, but—"

"Promise again!"

Georgina met her eyes for a long moment, then sighed. "I promise."

"Good. And thank you. I must be starting back to town now. I will be late for dinner as it is." Marianne turned back toward the road.

"Won't you think it over and come to see me again?" asked Georgina, hurrying to keep up with the other's long strides.

"There is nothing to think about."

"But . . ."

Marianne stopped abruptly, causing Georgina to collide with her. She turned and grasped both Georgina's hands, gazing earnestly into her face. "I thank you for being such a good friend," she said, "but there is nothing more to be said on this head. I hope you will simply forget it."

"I couldn't!"

"Well, put it from your mind, then. I intend to."

Georgina frowned, trying to think of some argument to sway her.

"And now I really must hurry. Will you be all right if I go on?"

"Of course," she responded automatically.

"Good-bye, then." And with a wave, Marianne departed, nearly running. In her haste, she did not once remember that she had also meant to talk to Georgina about Baron Ellerton.

Georgina followed more slowly, pondering what she had learned and racking her brain for some way to make it right. But her promise bound her to reluctant silence. Would not Marianne thank her if she broke it? she wondered. And yet she had been so vehement. Her forehead creased with this dilemma, Georgina returned to the inn.

13

Ellerton's visitors were still with him when Georgina returned to the inn, so she went directly upstairs and sat down in her bedchamber to think. She had always prided herself on her honesty and trustworthiness, but the current problem seemed to bring these into conflict. If she was honest with William in a matter which could decide his life's happiness, she would betray Marianne's trust. And though she felt that such a betrayal might be best for both in this situation, she could not make up her mind to it. Marianne had been angry, and revealing her confidences might simply make her more so. Georgina might make matters worse, she thought, by sending William to make an offer that Marianne refused out of pique and annoyance at her.

There seemed no satisfactory solution. Georgina was called down to dinner in the same state of mind, and ate abstractedly, paying no attention to the remarks of the landlady when she served, and thereby almost offending that kindly woman. She finished without any idea of what she had eaten and returned to her room in the same state. She did not go to the baron. Jenkins would be with him by now, serving his dinner and later readying him for sleep. Georgina's duties ended with dinnertime.

She tried to read, but her thoughts kept coming back to her two young friends and the question of the best way to help them. Considering both their characters, Georgina thought they might suit one another very well. The match would be a bit unequal in the world's terms, but not unduly so; Marianne would rouse William's liveliness and sense of fun, and William would provide a bulwark and useful channels for her energy. Smiling at her solemn wisdom, Georgina said aloud, "And they are obviously in love, which of course counts for something."

But this brought her no closer to deciding what to do. At last she concluded that she must talk to Marianne again, since she was forbidden to speak to William. Perhaps, when her temper had cooled, she would be more amenable to Georgina's suggestions. Thus, just before going to bed, Georgina wrote a note to be carried to the MacClain house first thing the following morning, asking Marianne to visit her again. This much settled, she was able to put the matter from her mind and fall asleep.

The following day dawned beautifully clear, without even the scattered clouds that had dotted the sky yesterday. Georgina woke to a breath of cool verdantly fresh air from her window, and as she rose and dressed and went down to breakfast she felt much more optimistic. Something would happen to make things right, she couldn't help believing, and when she gave her note to one of the stableboys to carry to town, she smiled so broadly that he was led to tell his fellows that the "nursing lady" was not so Friday-faced after all.

Ellerton was alone in the downstairs parlor when she sought him out. Jenkins had seen to his needs and helped carry him down before going off to bed,

Georgina was told when she inquired. "He looked dead beat," the baron added. "I've told him over and over that there is no need to sit up all night. I'm on the mend and unlikely to take a fit and wander off. But he won't listen. Sometimes, you know, I feel that I exist for the sake of my servants, rather than the other way about." He smiled to show that this was a joke, and when Georgina did not respond, added, "You are far away this morning." She did not seem to hear, and Ellerton examined her face more closely, realizing that he had become accustomed to their daily conversations, and looked forward to them. Georgina's viewpoint was, like his own, interestingly slanted, and the two were at the same time different enough to make her insights fascinating. He had met his match for the first time. She shared his interest in human nature and powers of observation, but her conclusions were slightly different—she saw what he did not and understood things he missed—thus adding to his knowledge and deepening his perceptions. Indeed, he realized, Georgina Goring was his counterpart, a thing he had not really expected to find in a woman. The fact had somehow crept up on him during these days, and emerged abruptly full blown.

Georgina, becoming conscious of the silence, looked up, startled, and said, "What?"

He merely smiled and shook his head.

"I'm sorry. I was thinking about something."

"Evidently. And something of compelling interest. What?"

"I can't . . ." Georgina hesitated. She could not, of course, tell him the whole story, but might she not give the outlines in order to ask his opinion? She had come to respect his judgments about people, for he seemed to sense things that she did not, often. "Two friends of mine have had a falling-out," she began haltingly. "They are, I believe, very dear to one another. Indeed, I think they might marry. But this . . . misunderstanding has separated them. One confided it to me, after making me promise that I would never speak of the circumstances, and when she had done so, I could see that it was nothing more than a muddle. I wished to speak to . . . my other friend, but she absolutely forbade it. It seems such a shame. I mean to talk to her again, to try to change her mind, but . . . What would you do?"

She raised clear gray eyes to his, her confidence in his perspicacity evident, and Ellerton felt an unexpected pang in the region of his heart. For a long moment he could only gaze at her delicately etched features, framed by pale blond curls and so full of sincerity and concern; then, seeing her begin to frown, he replied, "I suppose I would speak to the second friend."

"Even though you had sworn not to do so?"

"Some promises are unreasonable."

She pondered this. "I don't believe I would want those who made promises to me to think so," she answered finally.

"You implied that the happiness of two people rests on your actions," he responded.

Georgina nodded slowly.

"Do you think a moral scruple should stand in your way, then?" Ellerton felt more interested in her answer than in the problem.

"It is not only that. M . . . my friend might be so angry at my interference that she would refuse him after all. Or I might put it badly, and ruin everything."

"That, I cannot allow," he said. "But it is true that

when one begins to take a hand in others' lives, the outcome is uncertain."

"Have you ever done so?" she asked, curious.

"Once or twice."

"And you regretted it," she accused.

He shrugged. "I must admit I did. But neither case was as clear-cut as yours seems to be."

Georgina looked down. "I don't believe such things are ever clear-cut. I think I must do as I had decided already." She sighed.

"Perhaps I could help," he offered.

Georgina raised her head, surprised. "You? How?"

"Well . . ." He couldn't think of any way. He had been moved to offer by her disappointment. It seemed very important that he justify her confidence in him. "I don't suppose you would tell me the whole story, and allow me to speak to the man?"

She smiled. "But in that case, I may as well tell him myself. I am still betraying a confidence."

"I had hoped you might overlook that." He smiled, and after a moment she smiled back. "You are very scrupulous," he added.

Something in his gaze held Georgina silent. It made her throat tight and her breath seem constricted.

"Indeed," he added, "I don't believe I have ever known a person so concerned for others and at the same time so conscious of their foibles. An admirable combination. It allows you to be compassionate without losing your sense of the ridiculous. I must strive to emulate you. I tend too much to the latter side."

This did nothing to restore Georgina's powers of speech. That the polished Baron Ellerton should try to be like her was too astonishing an idea. Georgina had always seen herself as a bit clumsy.

His blue eyes started to twinkle. "I shall, however, strive to maintain my voice."

Acutely conscious of her lapse, Georgina blurted, "It is just so ... strange. That *you* should say such things to me."

"That *I*? What do you mean?"

"Well, you are so ... grand. I mean, I am awkward in company, and ... oh, I don't know. You see?"

"I'm not sure that I do." His expression was wry. "But I believe I've been insulted."

Georgina shook her head, aghast.

"To be called 'grand.' It calls up visions that make one shudder."

"I didn't mean it that way. Not that you look down your nose, but ..."

"Thank God for that, at least."

"You are just so ... so ..." Georgina paused, with no idea how to finish this sentence or repair her gaffe.

"I see I must make a determined effort to convince you of my sterling worth," he said, half-serious, half-teasing. "And I find I have a strong desire to do so."

"I think your character is ..." began Georgina, ready to say more than perhaps was wise to repair her mistake. But at this inopportune moment, Jenkins entered the room.

The valet looked from one to the other of them suspiciously in the charged silence that followed his appearance. He sensed that something was in the air, but he could not tell what. "I came to see about luncheon, my lord," he said then. "And I believe Miss Goring's is waiting downstairs. What would you like today?"

"Don't you ever sleep, man?" was the baron's reply. Jenkins drew back, startled.

Georgina, embarrassed by his hostile scrutiny as well as her own emotional state, turned and fled, flinging, "I must go," over her shoulder. Both men watched her, Ellerton annoyed and Jenkins indignant.

Georgina took her time over her meal, using it to regain her composure and rehearse the scene just past. Baron Ellerton had been amusing himself, she decided—not exactly at her expense, but he had meant nothing by it. He had probably thought she would laugh with him, and the next time, she would. And it was probably time that she thought of returning to town. It was obvious that Ellerton would recover completely; indeed, he would soon be able to travel to London himself. She had repaid Susan's carelessness to the full, and if in the process she had suited herself, it was now clear that she had gone far enough. She could no longer trust her emotions, and it would be wise to leave before she made a worse mistake than today.

Having come to this very sensible conclusion, Georgina immediately felt dispirited. She rose from the table determined to walk a little before going back upstairs. She was reluctant to face the baron again. But she had just gotten her hat and stepped outdoors when she was hailed from the road and turned to find Susan, William, and Tony riding up, grinning and waving.

"Hallo!" called Tony. "We've brought you another cargo of books. I don't know how you get through so many of them so quickly." A mass of tangled brown fur shot out from behind his horse and raced toward Georgina. "Here, now, Growser," shouted Tony. "Sunday manners!"

Though this did not stop the dog, he did not, as Georgina expected, throw himself upon her. He merely ran round and round barking joyfully and wriggling with apparent delight at seeing her again.

"We thought he would like the exercise," said Tony, dismounting nearby. "Here, sir, to me." Growser jumped up and sought to lick his master's face, reducing Tony to desperate defense of his primrose pantaloons.

William and Susan also climbed down, handing all three horses to an ostler. Georgina noticed a basket over Susan's arm. "You haven't brought Daisy!" she exclaimed.

Susan looked thunderous, as if she had heard this before. "Yes. Why shouldn't I?"

"Well, don't take him inside. Baron Ellerton will wring his neck."

"I should like to see him try!" retorted Susan.

"So should I," seconded Tony appreciatively.

Susan turned toward the inn, disgusted. Tony followed, keeping a grip on Growser, and Georgina fell in beside William. "How are you?" she said.

"Well," he replied in a voice that implied the opposite to one who knew him.

"Are you enjoying the Season still?"

"Susan is having a splendid time," was his evasive answer.

Georgina saw that she would get nothing from him without direct confrontation, and since she could not yet bring herself to this, she let it drop. They came into the inn and the leading pair started for the stairs. "The baron is in this parlor," said Georgina, stopping before the closed door. "He is much better."

"He can walk already?" exclaimed William.

"No, he is carried. Let me just see if he has finished . . ." But as soon as she opened the door, Growser was through it.

They heard, "What the devil?" from inside, and all four hurried after.

Ellerton was alone in the room. Growser stood with his front paws on the sofa cushions, examining him with scientific curiosity. The baron seemed torn between laughter and surprise. "Ah," he said when they came in, "this, I suppose, is another of Miss Wyndham's pets. What does he do? Eat one's waist-coats?"

"Growser is Tony's dog," protested Susan.

"Ah," said Ellerton again.

"And he don't bite," Tony assured him. "Though as for waistcoats . . ." He stopped, seeming to con-template some past incident.

The baron burst out laughing. "Remove him from my sofa, at least. Have you forgotten I am an invalid?"

As Tony pulled the dog away and pointed him toward the far corner of the room, William said, "You look much better, sir."

But Ellerton was not attending. His eyes were fixed upon the basket over Susan's arm. "Do not tell me that is—"

'I brought Daisy because he needed some fresh air," interrupted Susan defiantly. "He is not allowed out in London." They all watched, fascinated, as she set the basket on the floor and opened the lid. At once, Daisy popped out, then stretched enormously on the parlor carpet.

"At least he did not come through the thing unscathed," commented the baron, noticing a num-ber of scratches in the cat's ginger fur.

Daisy turned his yellow eyes on Ellerton and went very still. The two stared at one another for a long moment, and Georgina braced herself to move if Daisy leapt. However, the cat merely turned disdainfully after a while and stalked over to join Growser.

"You're the first person I've ever seen stare him down, Baron," said Tony, laughing.

"I was thinking of my neckcloth," responded Ellerton gloomily, causing Georgina to laugh as well.

"Daisy was just frightened," put in Susan. "It wasn't his fault."

"I don't blame your *cat*," answered the baron, fixing her with a stern eye.

Susan straightened and looked resolutely at the wall above his head. "I know it was my doing," she stated, as if giving a memorized speech. "I was very wrong, and I came today to beg your pardon. I will never do anything like that again."

"You will never get the chance with *me*," responded Ellerton. "But let us forget the whole matter. I accept your apology."

Susan looked both relieved and annoyed at his manner.

"Why don't you all sit down," suggested the baron. "I am developing a stiff neck looking up at you." They all quickly found chairs. "And so, how are you getting on? Is the Season up to your expectations?"

Susan chatted for a while about the parties she had attended and the people she had met, occasionally seconded by Tony. It became gradually apparent that William was not speaking at all. Ellerton, noticing this, caught Georgina watching the boy with great concern. His incipient boredom dissipated, and his eyes narrowed in thought. At the first pause in the conversation, he asked, "Where is Lady Marianne? Does she not usually accompany you on these visits?" He had heard as much from Georgina.

"Oh, she had another engagement," answered Susan lightly. "She is very busy." There was a hint of puzzlement in her voice, and this, combined with her brother's distinct start when Lady Marianne's name was mentioned, told Ellerton what he wanted to know.

"She's always flitting about someplace or other," added Tony. "We scarcely see her these days."

"I see her," protested Susan. She turned to Georgina. "Marianne has done just as you asked. She always invites me to accompany her and her family."

Georgina nodded, a little surprised that Susan would make a point of reassuring her.

"Well, William and I scarcely see her, though I live in the same house, eh, William?"

"I'm sure Lady Marianne has more important things to do," answered William, his voice expressionless.

Ellerton, certain now, merely smiled and turned the subject.

The three stayed for nearly an hour, the conversation sustained mainly by Susan and Tony, with questions from Georgina and, rarely, Baron Ellerton. Daisy and Growser lay in remarkable quiet in the corner. When Ellerton marveled at this, Tony simply shrugged, saying, "*I* don't understand it."

Finally Susan rose and said they must go. "I promised to be back at four," she told Georgina. "I am to have a new ball gown, and I must go for a fitting."

Tony hooted, but the two young men also stood.

"Do you need anything, Georgina?" asked William.

"No. I shall be returning to town soon, I think, and I have all I need until then." This was difficult to say, but, she told herself, necessary.

Ellerton turned to stare at her, but his quick movement went unnoticed in the round of farewells. The party was starting through the doorway when he recalled himself to say, "Wyndham, could I speak to you for a moment?"

They all stopped and turned again, surprised.

"A small matter," added the baron, his expression bland.

Looking puzzled, William stayed behind as the others filed out.

"If you would just shut the door," said Ellerton, and, totally bewildered, William did so. "Good. Now, I have something to say to you, which you may not wish to hear from me. Nonetheless, I think you will be grateful for the information."

"If it is about Susan—" began the younger man.

"It is not."

William stared at him, unable to imagine what Ellerton could have to say to him that required a closed door and such a serious tone.

"I know of no gradual way of leading up to this," the baron went on, feeling more awkward than he had expected, "so I will simply say it. You are in love with Lady Marianne MacClain."

William's mouth dropped open.

"And she is in love with you."

His blue eyes bulged with disbelief.

"You have had some sort of quarrel. I don't know the details, and don't care to. But if you have any sense at all, you will make it up and offer for her. This isn't a time for pride."

William made a strangled noise in his throat.

"You may think it odd that I bring up this matter . . ."

"She . . . she didn't *tell* you?" choked William, aghast at the idea that this elegant near-stranger knew of his despicable conduct.

"I have not spoken to Lady Marianne."

"But how . . . ?" This seemed to William some sort of magic, and he had not sufficiently gathered his wits to take in what he had been told.

"That doesn't matter. Be assured that I am telling you the truth. And don't, for God's sake, be a fool. Marry the girl!" Ellerton felt both ridiculous and compassionate. He could fully understand how shaken William must be, yet now that he had done what he set out to, he wished the boy would leave and put an end to this uncomfortable conversation. Ellerton was not accustomed to the role of mentor, and he did not find it easy.

"Sir," said William, regaining some measure of his composure, "I have no idea how you—"

"Nor are you likely to," interrupted the baron, his impatience to have this over now overriding politeness. "I've said what I meant to; there's no more to discuss."

"But I—"

"In fact, I'm rather tired," he added cravenly. "If you will excuse me."

William hadn't the address to do more than bow and take his leave, but he returned to his friends with his mind in turmoil. The baron's assurance that Marianne loved him was just sinking in, sweeping aside the mystery of how Ellerton had known anything about this matter. And the possibility was so thrilling that William lost himself in the realms of fantasy, forgetting to bid Georgina good-bye and failing to respond to the remarks Susan and Tony addressed to him. Fortunately, they were soon involved in one of their endless disputes, and took no more notice of William than he of them.

14

For William, the journey back to town passed in a daze. He went over and over Ellerton's remarks, pausing always at "she is in love with you." The phrase made him want to kick his horse to a gallop, whoop his happiness to the skies, and throw his hat into the air. The fact that he could do none of these things without lengthy explanations to his companions reduced him to a state of trembling tension, which transferred to his mount and caused it to shy and toss its head at the least excuse.

He wanted only to find Marianne and speak, yet when he thought of calling on her, some of his former nervousness returned. Did Baron Ellerton really know her feelings? he wondered. He could not believe the man would have spoken to him if he had not been certain. With this, William was assailed by remorse over his own behavior. What must Marianne think of him? It was no wonder she had been avoiding him, he thought. He had concluded that she was angry, but it now seemed that she might be hurt. This idea goaded him to near-frenzy. He had to see her at once.

They had reached the streets of London by this time, and were nearing the section where both the Goring and MacClain houses lay. William looked around, then said, "Let us go this way. We will pass Tony's house and can leave him there."

Tony looked surprised. "I thought you and I were to go on to Renfield's lodgings, to see about that horse of his."

"Oh." William had naturally forgotten about this previous engagement. "I believe I shall put him off. I'm . . . a little tired."

Susan gaped at him. "Are you joking? Besides, I want to get home as soon as possible. It's shorter that way." She pointed to a street that indeed led more directly to the Goring house, without passing Marianne's.

"We must be polite and accompany Tony," tried William, feeling himself on weak ground.

The other two were predictably amazed. Tony customarily rode home alone from their joint outings. "What's the matter with you?" asked Tony. "You've scarcely said a word the whole day, and now you seem to have gone off your head."

"There's nothing the matter," retorted William, and before they could object further, he turned his horse's head and moved in his chosen direction.

His friends hesitated, Susan appearing ready to go her own way without him, but finally they followed, shaking their heads at one another and frowning.

It was not far to the MacClain town house. William approached it as he might a five-barred gate on the hunting field, but drew up short when he discovered that Marianne was actually before him, being helped down from a showy carriage by a pink of the *ton*.

For a moment he was transfixed. Susan and Tony, coming up behind him, greeted Marianne and her escort, whom they had met before. The driver bowed and began an elaborate salutation; Marianne seemed immobile.

"I must speak to you!" blurted William, his blue eyes fixed on Marianne.

Her escort, cut off in mid-phrase, drew himself up and stared.

"It is very important," added William, conscious of nothing but her.

Susan and Tony were gaping as well by this time.

"As you see," managed Marianne in an unsteady voice, "I am engaged with Mr. Ottington."

William turned his gaze on her companion. Ottington, who had been ready to resent this high-handed intrusion, saw something in Wyndham's eyes that made him shrink back. "Just returning, actually," he stammered. "Been driving in the park. Harmless, you know. Must be getting on." He grasped Marianne's hand before she could offer it, bowed again, and turned to his vehicle. In another moment he was driving away, leaving behind a startled, silent group.

William dismounted. "Would you see Susan home, Tony?" he requested.

"I thought *you* were escorting me home?" protested his friend, more bewildered than put out.

"Please," replied William, throwing him a speaking glance.

"Have you gone mad?" said his sister. "I have never seen you behave so oddly in your life."

William simply made a dismissive gesture, his attention focused on Marianne, and Tony bent to take the rein of Susan's horse. "Come on."

"But I don't—"

"Let him be," advised Tony. He had the sense that something significant was going forward, though he was not clear just what.

Marianne watched the two ride off, and William watched her profile. When they disappeared around a corner, and she turned, he said, "Shall we go inside?"

"This is very inconvenient," answered Marianne. "I am going out to dinner, and I must—"

"It won't take long. Please, Marianne."

She eyed him. His expression was most unsettling. A dreadful suspicion entered her mind. "Where have you been? Have you been talking to your cousin?"

"Georgina? No." William was surprised by her evident concern. "We have been visiting the baron, but I barely spoke to Georgina."

"What do you want?" responded Marianne, more composed.

"To talk with you for five minutes."

"Go on, then."

"We cannot talk in the street."

"Why not? I cannot imagine what you may have to say to me that cannot—"

"Marianne!"

His tone made her stop abruptly, and sent a shiver down her spine. "Very well!" She whirled and rang the bell. The door was opened so quickly that those more capable of observation might have suspected an eavesdropper. But William and Marianne were beyond such considerations. William thrust the reins of his mount into the outraged footman's hand and strode after her into the library.

"Well, what is it?" she asked when he had shut the door behind him. "I did not think we had anything more to say to one another."

Now that he had a clear field, William found that his tongue clove to the roof of his mouth. She was so beautiful, and so obviously angry with him, that he could not think how to begin. "Shall we sit down?" he managed feebly.

Marianne glared at him, then sat in an armchair before the fireplace. He moved slowly to the chair opposite, marshaling his thoughts. There was a short silence.

"I really must go upstairs," said Marianne. She was mystified by his reticence, following so soon after his insistence on coming in. When she had first seen him ride up, her heart had begun to pound, and when he had demanded to speak to her, a flame of hope had risen. It had taken all her self-control to assume cool indifference, but she was very glad of it now. Had he come simply to offer another idiotic apology?

"I am finding it difficult to start," said William, "perhaps because I know what a fool I have been, and I am afraid to repeat my mistakes."

This was so interesting that Marianne unconsciously dropped her indifferent pose.

"The other day, on our ride, I . . . I did behave badly," he went on.

Marianne stiffened again.

"Partly in giving way to my feelings, and partly in not then telling you of them." He swallowed. "Frankly, I was a coward. I was afraid to tell you that I love you and wish with all my heart to make you my wife. I thought you would surely refuse."

Marianne went very still.

"When I was berating myself for my lapse, you see, I was overwhelmed by the disparity of our positions. You could make a far better match from a worldly point of view, and indeed, I knew that you had refused a brilliant alliance, so I . . ." he ran down. As he stated the case, he nearly succeeded in again convincing himself that his suit was hopeless.

Marianne felt a wave of highly inappropriate giggles rising in her chest. When he said he loved her, she had at first felt as if a great burden had been lifted from her soul, leaving joy in its wake. But as he went on, tangling himself further and further in rationalization, her feelings threatened to erupt in laughter. This, she knew, would be inexcusable, but she could not resist saying, "Do you *wish* me to refuse you?"

"What? No!"

"You are arguing against yourself so insistently."

"I wasn't. I didn't mean . . . it is just that I am so conscious of the inequality of—"

"But why mention it? *If*, that is, you truly wish to convince me."

William looked at her, pained. He had not imagined, when he heard that she loved him, that his proposal would be so difficult. He almost wished he had not spoken at all. "I wish with all my heart to marry you," he replied. "I can say no more than that."

Taking pity on him, and unable to restrain her own happiness any longer, Marianne smiled. "Yes."

"What?" He seemed uncertain he had heard correctly.

"Yes," repeated Marianne, "I will marry you."

"But . . . but . . ."

"There! I said you did not mean it."

William jumped to his feet in distress. "Marianne! I did. I do! I was just . . ."

"When a man apologizes so profusely for kissing one, after all . . ." She shrugged and raised her eyebrows, laughter close to the surface.

This was too much. William took one step forward

and grasped her elbows, jerking her to her feet. Then his arms slid around her and pulled her against him as his lips met hers in a passionate kiss.

Before Marianne could really respond, he drew back, holding her by the shoulders at arm's length. "There! I shan't apologize for *that*."

She gazed at him, her laughter swept away by very different feelings. "Good."

"In fact, I shall do it again." And he did.

This time, Marianne had ample time to put her arms around his neck and second his efforts whole-heartedly. Their bodies pressed closer, and both lost themselves in sensation, forgetting the rest of the world. An eternity seemed to pass as they wordlessly communicated a host of things that neither had yet said aloud.

Finally they drew apart again, though not far. Marianne smiled up at him. "A man may after all," he said, "kiss his promised wife."

"He is practically obliged," she answered.

William eyed her. "Has anyone ever told you that you joke at the most inappropriate times?"

"Heaps of people," was the cheerful reply. "Since I was tiny."

He smiled. "And have you never thought they might be right?"

"No. They were usually such *solemn* people."

"Ah." He frowned. "Do you think I am too solemn?"

"Do you think I am too frivolous?"

"You are perfect!"

Marianne laughed at last. "And so are you, in a different way."

"I suppose we can learn from one another. But I shall never be a jokster, Marianne." He looked doubtful.

"No, but you will become much better at *taking* a joke, I'm sure."

"So I am to be your butt?"

"Naturally. I shall devote all my time to discovering ways to mock you."

William frowned, then saw the teasing twinkle in her blue eyes and smiled again. "You will certainly not lack opportunities," he replied ruefully.

"William! I was only funning. I should never mock you." She hesitated. "Exactly."

"And what 'exactly' will you do?"

She met his gaze squarely. "Be your wife, and love you with all my heart."

There could be only one answer to this, and William gave it very willingly. It was nearly twenty minutes before the couple emerged, beaming, from the library and stood before the front door together.

"I will call on your mother at nine," William said, holding her hand and gazing fondly down on her.

"All right." Marianne grinned. "I will prepare her for your visit."

"Do you think she will need bracing?"

"I think she will need to be told beforehand what is afoot, or she will pay no attention to what you are saying." She laughed a little.

After a moment, William followed suit.

"I will write to my brother by the next post. I suppose he and Alicia will come racing back to see what I am up to."

William looked concerned. "Shall I write to him also? I could explain my situation and—"

"Nonsense. Mama is my guardian."

"I hope to be friends with your brother, however," he chided gently.

"Oh, Ian will *adore* you!"

He laughed again. "Why do I feel that is not a compliment?"

"It is. More or less."

William looked inquiring.

"Ian and I have not always agreed, and I still rather enjoy startling him. I can't help but regret a little that we shall agree completely on *you*."

"Shall I lose my fortune at hazard or fight a duel so that he will disapprove of me?" Marianne looked pensive. "Stay! That was my own feeble idea of a joke."

She dimpled. "I know. And a promising one. The thought is tempting, though."

"Not to me!"

"Oh, well, you would probably do it backward. Your dice would never fall wrong, and you would challenge the greatest blackguard in England and rid the country of him, earning general thanks."

"Marianne!" He was half-laughing, half-scandalized.

She wrinkled her nose at him. "I *must* go and change. They will be waiting dinner for me."

He nodded. "Until tonight, then."

"Yes."

Seeing that the hall was empty, he kissed her lightly again and took his leave. Marianne walked slowly up the stairs to her bedchamber, a dreamy smile making her even more lovely than usual.

15

All was formally settled between Marianne and William later that evening, when he called after the family's return from a dinner party. There could be no objection to the Wyndham lineage or fortune, and Lady Bentham made none. She had satisfied herself of Marianne's happiness in a private talk, and she asked nothing more. The newly engaged couple spent a happy hour drafting a notice for the *Morning Post*, and an even more agreeable period discussing their future and bidding one another a very fond farewell. It was settled that William would come to dinner the following evening and become better acquainted with Lady Bentham and her husband.

These arrangements complete, Marianne had the leisure, as she was getting ready for bed, to wonder again how their reconciliation had been effected. She had forgotten, in the general excitement, to press William for information, so she determined to rise early and visit Georgina, the most probable agent of the change.

She arrived at the posting house by ten, having left home right after breakfast, and she found Georgina again setting out for a walk in the countryside.

"Baron Ellerton has visitors," she replied when asked about her patient's progress. "I have not seen him since yesterday, but he is mending quickly now. Dr. Mason gave him crutches."

"Good." Marianne's reply was perfunctory. "May I come with you once again?"

"If you are certain you do not prefer to go inside."

Shaking her head, Marianne fell in beside the older woman, and they walked for a while in silence. Georgina had just formulated her argument about William when Marianne said, "I came partly to bring you some good news."

"Yes?"

"William and I are engaged."

"What?" Georgina stopped and clasped her hands together. "Oh, Marianne, that is wonderful. But how did it come about? When we spoke last time . . ."

Marianne, who had been carefully watching her face for signs of previous knowledge, was disappointed. She would have sworn that her revelation was a complete surprise to Georgina. "He came to me yesterday afternoon and apologized." She grinned. "Indeed, he rather *over*apologized. And then he made an offer."

"I am so glad! But what can have caused William . . . that is . . . Never mind." Georgina realized too late that her puzzlement over William's move was hardly flattering. Yet her knowledge of William's character made her wonder what had impelled him. He was too modest to have acted without urging, she was sure.

Marianne laughed. "That is exactly what I came to ask you. In fact, I am tempted to accuse you of interference." She was watching the other's expression closely again. "Not that I could scold you too harshly for it, since it brought me such happiness."

Georgina shook her head, frowning. "I did not

speak to him. I thought of it, and I wished to, but I could not make up my mind to betray a confidence."

Marianne believed her. No one could feign such perplexed ignorance, she decided. "Did you mention my story to anyone else? But no, you would not."

"No," said Georgina, then abruptly remembered her careful conversation with Ellerton.

"Well, perhaps William did it on his own," continued Marianne, oblivious now of the arrested look on her companion's face. "I like that even better. One doesn't particularly like to feel that one's affianced husband had to be goaded to his proposal."

Georgina made a vaguely affirmative sound, absorbed in her own thoughts.

Marianne was now equally intent. "We are to be married at the end of the Season. William is taking me down to meet his mother in two weeks, when his brother will be at home as well. I wrote to Ian, too. He will be astonished by my prudent choice." Turning to share this mild joke, she finally noticed Georgina's distance. "What is it? Have you thought of something?"

"Umm? Oh, no, nothing. I was just thinking how you will like Anabel, and she you." Georgina was not yet ready to share her theory. The suspicion that Ellerton had taken this kindly task on himself had affected her deeply, and she wanted to assimilate the fact herself before passing it on.

"William's mother? I hope she will. I am a little uneasy about that visit, actually."

This captured Georgina's full attention. "But why?"

Marianne looked at the ground. "You may not have heard—the talk of last year is died down now— but my father was . . . a notorious rake. I told William; he doesn't care. But his family might . . ."

"Anabel won't give a snap of her fingers for your father," Georgina assured her. "And neither will Christopher—her husband, you know. They will judge you as you are, and they will love you at once."

"Do you think so?"

"I am positive."

Marianne heaved a sigh. She had been more concerned about this than she realized.

"Will you be married in London?" asked Georgina, to divert her.

She nodded. "Scotland is too far, and besides, most of my friends are here." She went on happily detailing the plans that had been made, and Georgina again relapsed into her own thoughts.

Ellerton might have worked out whom she meant, Georgina decided, especially considering William's transparent unhappiness during his visit. She remembered then that the baron had kept William back to speak to him privately, and her suspicion became a certainty. Baron Ellerton had brought William and Marianne together because of her talk with him.

For some reason, this knowledge filled Georgina was a warm glow. She was merely pleased, she told herself, that her cousin and her friend had surmounted the barriers to their happiness. But she could not deny that the *means* of their reconciliation was particularly gratifying. The baron's intervention had been so disinterested and so benevolent; she rejoiced to think of him in such terms. The doubts she had sometimes felt about his capacity for feeling—when his interest in others had seemed merely intellectual—dissolved. He was a thoroughly admirable character, she told herself blissfully. It was at this point that Marianne mentioned the baron's name, effectively capturing Georgina's attention again. "What?" she said, looking up.

Marianne looked self-conscious. "Don't be offended. I only wish to help. And I daresay you know everything I am going to say very well, and have considered it already."

"I don't know what you're talking about," admitted Georgina, who had lost the thread of the conversation.

Marianne bit her lower lip. "You mean that I have no business giving you advice. That is true, of course. I just do not want to see you ... perhaps embarrassed by a mistaken impression."

"Marianne, I vow I don't know what you mean."

The younger girl looked at her. "I am talking about Baron Ellerton, of course."

Georgina simply frowned.

"Oh, come. It was obvious when you determined to stay and nurse him, even after his servants arrived, that you ... felt an unusual interest in him. I only wanted to say that he is much pursued, and you should not, well, form false hopes or ..." Marianne broke off in confusion, wishing she had never begun. She felt ridiculous admonishing this woman who was both years older and much more reserved than she.

Georgina felt as if she were falling from the heights of fantasy to a most unwelcome reality. Her joy in Ellerton's kindness was overwhelmed by the truth of Marianne's assertion, and all her doubts came rushing back. Whatever the baron did, it had nothing to do with her. She had, perhaps, piqued his interest with her tale of thwarted love, and he had indeed shown his quality in untangling the situation, but Georgina's part in it was mere informant, just as her relationship with Ellerton was no more than mild friendship, if that. He was, naturally, grateful for her help, and they occasionally shared a moment of amused understanding, but this was no basis for the rush of feeling Georgina had experienced a few moments before. She was, she thought unhappily, doing just what Marianne sought to warn her against. She was building upon her artificial intimacy with Ellerton when it was in fact a temporary, and meaningless, coincidence.

"Oh, how I wish I had not opened my mouth," exclaimed Marianne. "Of course you know what you are about. I mean . . . I was just—"

"It doesn't matter," interrupted Georgina, her voice sounding flat in her own ears. "You needn't worry about me."

"No," agreed Marianne, relieved that Georgina seemed neither angry at her nor unduly upset by her remarks. She must have been mistaken, she told herself. Georgina did not care for Baron Ellerton after all.

Her duty done, Marianne gladly turned the subject to more pleasant things, and they finished their walk in further discussion of her plans. By the time she took her leave some half-hour later, Marianne had nearly forgotten about the baron, and she rode back to London immersed in her own happiness, so abstracted that her groom more than once had to warn her of a hazard in the road.

Georgina reentered the inn to hear that Ellerton's visitors from London had departed and that he had asked for her. But she did not go to him immediately. She slipped upstairs to her own bedchamber and sat down in the armchair near the window, looking out over the garden behind the inn and trying to regain her customary calm.

But instead of growing more composed, she became steadily less so. In Marianne's presence, Georgina had held her feelings in check, but alone, she could give them free play. Indeed, she could do nothing else, for they were too strong.

She had been exceedingly stupid, she thought miserably. She had ignored her own inner warnings during these days away from society, and she had unconsciously assumed that Baron Ellerton was feeling as she did—content and happy in her company and increasingly drawn to her, as she, she admitted now, was to him. Despite Jenkins' cautionary tales, and her own common sense, she had fallen in love with him.

This revelation brought tears to Georgina's eyes. How could she have been so foolish? she wondered. She had always prided herself on the sharpness of her intellect, but in this she had acted directly against its strictures; she had no one to blame but herself.

The best thing to do, that sensible part of herself declared, was to leave, as she had determined before. Back in her aunt's town house, with Susan's antics and William's joyful plans to occupy her, she would no doubt soon forget the baron. Her youthful infatuation had passed off in a matter of months when she had determinedly turned her attention elsewhere. When she saw Susan's stepfather now, she rarely even thought of the time she had fancied herself in love with him. This would be the same.

But another part of her remained stubbornly unconvinced. This was *not* the same, it insisted. This love was not built on the imaginings of a schoolgirl, and though its foundation might be equally illusory, the result was not. She would not forget Ellerton, ever.

A knock at the door made Georgina jump, her

heart pounding. It was a moment before she could call, "Yes?"

Her maid looked in. "His lordship is calling for you, miss. Should I tell him that you're resting?"

Georgina rose and came forward. "No, I'll go down now." She would have to see him eventually, she told herself as she followed the girl downstairs to the parlor, and thinking was merely making her more agitated. She did not admit that his asking for her had raised a tiny hope.

The baron was reading one of her books when she came in, stretched out on the sofa with a mug of ale nearby. In the moment before he looked up, Georgina gazed lingeringly at his face. He was more than handsome to her now, she thought. She could see there all the qualities she admired.

He raised his head, and their eyes met. Georgina found it suddenly difficult to breathe. "Ah, there you are," he said, his voice very cool. "Where have you been? Packing your things?"

This took Georgina by surprise, and she merely looked at him.

"You did say yesterday that you would be leaving soon," he added, "so when I didn't see you today, I assumed you were making ready to go."

"You had visitors," blurted Georgina.

"Yes, of course." His tone implied boredom, but in actuality, Ellerton was furious. He had been taken by surprise by Georgina's statement the previous day. He had not thought of her leaving, and his first reaction was denial. He did not wish her to go. And it was somehow worse that she had not discussed the matter with him first, but had simply presented it, in company, as a fact. And then she had disappeared. Jenkins had brought his dinner and, as usual, remained with him through the evening and night, and at the hour when Georgina customarily joined him after breakfast, a pack of chattering Londoners turned up. Ellerton had sent them on their way as soon as he decently could, but even then, Georgina had stayed away. When he was forced to send for her, the baron's temper worsened further. "Well, do you intend to tell me your plans?" he went on, some emotion in his voice now. "Or were you going to simply depart and leave me to discover it for myself?"

"I didn't . . . I wasn't . . ."

"Not, of course, that you have any particular obligation to me. You have done a great deal too much already. Jenkins and the others can look after me quite well."

His manner seemed to confirm Georgina's worst fears. He didn't want her here, she concluded. When he had been too ill to care who attended him, it had not mattered, but now he was weary of her constant presence, and using her own reluctant words as an excuse to be rid of her. The idea was very painful, but she refused to show it. "It is time I was getting back to town," she agreed, her voice shaking only a little. "Susan needs me, especially now that William is to be married. He is engaged to Lady Marianne, you know."

This news diverted the baron briefly. "Is he?"

"Yes." Georgina gathered all her courage; whatever her own feelings, she was determined to thank him for his part in that affair. "That was your doing, I think. I am very grateful to you."

"You figured that out, did you?" He looked at her more kindly, impressed yet again by her powers of observation and quick understanding.

"It could have been no one else. It was so kind of you."

"Merely pursuing my interest in human nature," he answered lightly, and smiled. For a moment the conversation hung in delicate balance. The old sympathy between them worked to dissipate the discord. But then the baron recalled his grievance. It seemed monstrously unfair that she should leave because of his own "kind" act. "And so you return to London to help with the wedding?" he asked sharply.

"I will certainly give what help I can," she replied unhappily. "Though it is Susan who will need me most, I imagine. The MacClains will be too busy to take her about."

"Ah." He could not argue against this, though had he known how much Georgina regretted her words, he might have done so. "When do you mean to leave?"

Somehow, Georgina thought miserably, she had maneuvered herself into a corner. While part of her protested violently, she responded, "This afternoon, unless you wish me to stay a day or two longer."

"No, indeed," he said through clenched teeth. "Jenkins will take things in hand."

"He'll be delighted to," added Georgina with a spark of wistful humor.

Ellerton had to smile. "He will."

She stood in silence before him. She could still change her mind, a part of her argued. She could find some excuse to stay. But the voice of reason was stronger now that he had, as Georgina thought, encouraged her to go. She would not hang about like one of those women the valet had described so vividly, waiting for the least crumb of attention, forcing herself on Ellerton when he could not get away. The fact that she loved him was humiliating enough without playing out such a pathetic charade. "I . . . I should pack." she said forlornly.

The baron was too wrapped up in his own resentment to hear the tone. "Of course," was his cool reply.

She turned to go.

"Miss Goring."

"Yes?" Georgina scolded herself for the eager hope she heard in the word.

"Since I suppose we will not be seeing one another for some time, I should thank you once again for the help you have given me."

Her spirits fell as quickly as they had risen. "It was nothing. I was . . . that is, Susan caused your accident, so it seemed only right."

"Nonetheless, I do thank you." Inwardly he cursed the heedless Susan. The woman cared for nothing but her damned cousins, he thought. Let her go to them!

Georgina made a dismissive gesture, as if to physically put off his thanks. She hesitated before turning toward the door again. He had seemed to imply that she was not to come back here. "Well," she ventured, "good-bye."

"Good-bye, Miss Goring." Ellerton's voice habitually grew more distant with intensity of emotion, so that by this time he sounded scarcely interested.

Georgina waited one more instant, wishing to speak but having nothing to say, then turned again and went out. Ellerton gazed at the empty doorway for a long time after she left it.

16

Georgina's packing did not take long. Most of her clothes were still in London, and Susan and William had been carrying books back and forth for her so that she had only a few in her possession. Her greatest problem was explaining to a startled Lucy the reasons for their sudden departure. The maid was full of questions for which she had no good answers, and finally she sent her down to ask the landlord about hiring a chaise simply to be rid of her.

But Lucy was back almost at once. "He says it's all right," she told Georgina. "They're harnessing up now."

"Oh." This was what Georgina had requested, but she realized then that she had had some lingering hope that she would be forced to stay by lack of a vehicle. She raised her chin. "Good. You can take the dressing case down now. And ask someone to fetch the other things."

"Yes, miss. I swear I had no idea we were going so soon. I —"

"I decided rather quickly, yes, Lucy. Go on now."

In what seemed to Georgina a remarkably short time, all was ready. The innkeeper urged her to eat a bite of luncheon before she set out, but she wasn't hungry. She allowed him to press a packet of sandwiches on her for Lucy's sake, and then urged the maid to climb up. At the last moment, she nearly balked and went to Ellerton, but the interested gazes of the landlord, ostlers, and others in the yard changed her mind. She was very close to tears, and she did not want to break down before all these curious strangers. Thus, she got in the chaise, and the driver signaled his team. Georgina did not even feel comfortable twisting round to watch the inn out of sight.

Inside the private parlor, Ellerton had no such qualms. Stretched out on the sofa, he had a clear view of Georgina's departure through a front window, and was secure in the knowledge that none could see in as well as he saw out. This was the only gratifying circumstance, however, and he was very pleased to see that Georgina did not look happy as she left.

But this pleasure was short-lived. When the chaise had disappeared around a bend in the road, and even the sound of its wheels had died away, Ellerton lay back on his pillows with a sigh. His anger was fading, and with Georgina gone, he had the leisure to consider his actions. They had been very odd, he concluded. Why had he flown into such a rage? It was inevitable that Georgina return to London in time, and surely he was not so selfish as to wish to keep her to provide amusement for himself now that he was better. He had visitors often, and the doctor was talking of letting him return to his own house.

Yet these reasonable assertions did nothing to dispel the regret he felt at her leaving. He remembered some of their conversations, a smile curving his lips, and suddenly envisioned her face as he had sometimes seen it, vivid with laughter. A most unusual woman, he concluded, with qualities one rarely found in anyone, male or female. He would look forward to seeing her again, in town.

But when Ellerton imagined that scene—a crowded drawing room, loud with chatter and smoky with candlelight—his heart sank. That was not what he wanted, he realized. He wanted to continue as they had been, alone, quietly talking and laughing over shared observations, near enough to accidentally brush hands. Without warning, he was filled with blinding desire for Georgina. All his senses came alive with memories of her, a series of glowing sensuous pictures flashing through his mind. At first, he was too astonished to do more than lie still, eyes wide, breath quickening, and then, in an instant, he saw that he loved her. His body had been too weakened by injuries to respond until now, and he had mistaken his feelings for something milder. But at this inopportune point, when she was out of reach, perhaps forever, he saw the truth. This was the woman he had searched for all his life, and he had sent her away.

But as he struggled to sit straighter, jarring his broken ribs, and started to call for Jenkins, Ellerton was shaken by a highly uncharacteristic doubt. Georgina had given no sign of feelings like these, he thought. She had been performing a duty, and she had gone as soon as it was done. Ignoring his own role in her departure, the baron hesitated. He had been ready to force Jenkins to hire a carriage and accompany him to London, and damn all doctors. But now he was uncertain. What if she should refuse him?

This was a novel thought for the much-sought-after Baron Ellerton. His efforts had been directed toward avoiding entanglement for years; it was odd to be not only contemplating marriage but also wondering whether his suit would be acceptable. And yet she *had* stayed, he told himself, and she had seemed to enjoy their times together.

Ellerton had a very unusual afternoon. He spent it arguing first one side and then the other of his dilemma, unaware of Jenkins bustling blissfully about his room or the other sounds of an active posting house. He could recall no other time in his life when he had felt so indecisive, and he did not care for the feeling at all. It had driven him nearly to distraction when Jenkins came in yet again and announced a visitor. "Sir William Wyndham, my lord."

William was directly on his heels. "The others are coming, sir," he blurted as soon as he was inside the parlor. "I rode ahead so that I could thank you for speaking to me yesterday. You may have heard that Marianne and I are to be married." At Ellerton's nod, he grinned and shrugged. "And it is all your doing. You were dead right. One can't let anything keep one from the girl one loves. I shall never be able to repay you for telling me that."

The baron was gazing at him fixedly. "Perhaps you will," he said slowly.

"What?" William looked mystified, but willing.

Ellerton considered a moment, then nodded. "I must get to London at once," he declared. "And you can help me. This damned leg won't let me ride. It must be a carriage, and slowly, I suppose."

"But I thought the doctor—"

"The doctor says you aren't to travel for at least a week, my lord," interrupted Jenkins indignantly. The valet had left the room when William arrived, but he had come back with a tray in time to hear Ellerton's request. "He said he can't guarantee that you'll heal

properly if you bounce about on the road just now,"
he went on. "And you won't while I'm alive!"

"Mason is being overcautious," snapped the baron.
"I feel much better."

"And didn't he say you would?" replied Jenkins.
"And that you'd likely get restless and try to move
before you should. No, my lord, I won't allow it."

Ellerton looked to William.

"I . . . I wouldn't want to do anything that would
prevent your recovery," stammered the younger man,
torn between gratitude and responsibility. "If the
doctor says—"

He was interrupted by the arrival of Susan, Tony,
and Marianne, full of high spirits and teasing him
about his neck-or-nothing riding on their approach
to the inn. It was some minutes before this died
away, time enough for the baron to stifle his rage and
William to conclude that he had done the right thing.
He could not, he decided, endanger Ellerton's health,
no matter what he owed him.

"Where is Georgina?" asked Marianne then. "She
will laugh at me for riding out twice in one day, but
William convinced me." The engaged couple gazed
fondly at one another.

"She has gone home," was the curt reply. "You
must have passed her carriage on your way."

"What?" They all looked astonished.

"She didn't tell us she was coming," accused Susan.
"And we *didn't* see her. She would have called out."

"It was probably that 'shortcut' you led us into,"
answered Tony. "Wasted half an hour, and made us
miss her. I *told* you that—"

"It did not!" protested Susan. "It was much quicker
than last time. But I suppose Georgina kept to the
main road."

"Of course she did." Tony was contemptuous.

"Well, we will see her at home," retorted Susan, and turned her back on him.

Marianne was frowning. "She said nothing this morning about going." She looked at Ellerton, her earlier concern returning twofold.

"A sudden decision," he answered in an indifferent voice. "But you must allow me to wish you happy, both of you."

This successfully diverted William, who never liked to think the worst. He led Marianne in a discussion of their wedding plans, and the question of Georgina was allowed to drop. Ellerton could see that Marianne was not satisfied, but he had no intention of allowing her to find out the truth. Yet this minor matter occupied only a small part of his attention, as did his visitors' chatter. His whole mind was bent on the burning question of how he was to get to London and see Georgina. A letter would not do, he had concluded. He felt he must see her and take his chance. For William's echo of his own words had tipped the balance of his indecision. He could not allow Georgina to slip away from him through his own inaction.

Ellerton felt imprisoned during the next half-hour. He was surrounded by jailers, with the best intentions in the world. How could he elude Jenkins and find aid in getting to town? he wondered over and over again. He would not be at all surprised to learn that Jenkins had alerted the inn servants to his plight. They would refuse to help him, no doubt. And he could not travel without assistance; he was not so foolish as that.

"They should let him do as he likes!" exclaimed

Susan Wyndham at that moment, in response to some remark of Tony's.

Ellerton had lost the thread of the conversation, but this statement captured his attention. He eyed Susan speculatively. She might well have sympathy with his powerlessness, and she owed him a very large debt. Some of the tension left his expression as he began to plan his campaign.

When the four young people rose to take their leave, Ellerton was ready. "Miss Wyndham, could I speak to you for a moment?" he asked. "Miss Goring left a message for you."

"For me?" Susan looked pleased to be thus singled out. "Of course." She waited as the others filed out, Marianne frowning. When William shut the parlor door, she gazed inquiringly at the baron.

"I fear that was a ruse, Miss Wyndham. What I wish to say to you does not concern your cousin." Though he realized at once that this was untrue, he pushed the thought aside. This must be left as uncomplicated as possible.

"If you are going to scold me again for driving your phaeton—" Susan began.

"I am not. It has nothing to do with that either. I need your help, Miss Wyndham."

"Mine?" She looked mystified, and a bit intrigued.

"I must go to London at once, and the servants here refuse to allow me to do so because of the doctor's orders." He had decided to be frank.

"The doctor is afraid you will hurt yourself more?" asked Susan.

"Yes. But he has said I may travel in a week, and doctors are always overcautious."

"That's true. When I had the measles, they made me stay in bed for days after I felt fine."

"Exactly. I will not be hurt, and it is vital I get to town."

She surveyed him speculatively. "Why?"

"That need not concern you. I think you owe me your aid, Miss Wyndham. I would *be* in London now if not for you."

Susan grimaced, then shrugged. "Oh, very well. What do you want me to do?"

For a moment Ellerton could not believe it was so easy; then he recovered and launched into his plan. Susan listened closely, nodding from time to time and seeming unconcerned with anything other than understanding what she must do. "You have it?" finished the baron.

"Yes. I'll come right after breakfast."

"Splendid! You are an unusual girl, Miss Wyndham."

She grinned impishly at him, and went out.

17

Once his plans were made, Ellerton relaxed and concentrated on carrying them through. His desire to see Georgina was undiminished, but he knew that certain steps must be accomplished first. His main problem was Jenkins, and he began at once to surmount it. He kept his valet running here and there on various errands through the evening, attempting, without seeming to, to wear him out. Then he forced himself to wake after a few hours' sleep and find new services his valet could perform. Ellerton had been sleeping soundly through the night since the end of the first week after his accident. Indeed, he had repeatedly told Jenkins that it was unnecessary for him to sit up. Now he was glad the man had resisted, for it gave him the opportunity to ensure his lack of alertness the next day.

By early morning, the baron was satisfied, and he managed another few hours' sleep during the time when Jenkins must be busy with the morning routine. When his valet brought the breakfast tray sometime later, Ellerton even felt a bit guilty, for Jenkins really did look exhausted. And it was with real sincerity in his voice that Ellerton urged him to go to bed.

"Perhaps I will, my lord," agreed the other, "for a

few hours. If you should want anything, you can always—"

"I shall be fine. Go on."

Picking up the tray to return it to the kitchen, Jenkins nodded. "I'll look in on you before luncheon, my lord."

Ellerton made an airy gesture. He mustn't be too emphatic, he knew, or Jenkins' easily aroused suspicions would surface. The valet went out, and he felt some of the tension ease. That hurdle seemed safely past. He had had Jenkins shave him, and he was fully dressed, as he always insisted on being lately. There was nothing to do now but wait for Susan to arrive, and hope that she hadn't botched it.

This time seemed very long to Baron Ellerton. He was accustomed to making his own arrangements and acting for himself, and in this vital matter he would have vastly preferred doing so. But as he had no alternative, he tried to school himself to patience. His success was limited. Do what he might, scenes of disaster continued to form in his brain—Jenkins discovering them as they were on the point of leaving, Susan failing to secure a carriage and avoiding telling him so, and more disagreeably, his injuries worsening irreparably because of the journey. Though he did not think the latter probable, the worry would intrude, and more than once he wondered if he was doing the right thing. But the pressure to see Georgina and settle things between them, for good or ill, was stronger than this concern. All his faculties were focused on getting to her; indeed, the one scene he did not visualize was that with her. The disaster of her refusal he could not contemplate.

At last, after what seemed hours to Ellerton, when he looked out the window at the sound of a carriage, it was Susan, and not some unknown traveler. He saw the girl get down from a hired chaise, speak briefly to the driver, and enter the inn. He swung his uninjured leg to the floor and prepared for the ordeal of moving.

In the next moment, Susan was looking round the door, her green eyes gleaming with mischief. "Are you ready?"

"Yes. Is the corridor clear?" Ellerton didn't want to meet any of his servants, or, if it could be avoided, the inn servants. None would oppose him like Jenkins, but there might be some dispute, and he did not wish to attract attention and the chance of someone recalling the doctor's orders.

Susan looked, then nodded.

"You will have to help me. The crutches are over there." The doctor had provided a pair of crutches, but as he had commanded they not be used for three days, they had been placed in the far corner of the room, where Ellerton could not reach them.

Susan fetched them quickly and helped the baron lever himself up and onto them. He tried them awkwardly, nearly falling. "Here," said Susan, "lean on my shoulder on one side. That will be steadier."

This worked better, and they made their way out of the parlor and into the hall, going more slowly than Ellerton would have liked. The strong wish for speed, combined with his inability to achieve it, was maddening.

"Does it hurt?" asked Susan, betraying more worry than either of them had expected.

"No," lied Ellerton. In fact, his leg was signaling distress, though the pain was not enough to seriously concern him. It was hardly more than the ache in his ribs when he breathed deeply.

They reached the front door and started outside, only to be nearly knocked over by an entering ostler. The man looked considerably startled to see Ellerton walking. The baron himself had to smile. He must look ridiculous, he realized, supported by a pair of sticks and a ravishingly pretty redhead.

They were halfway across the innyard to the chaise when the voice of the innkeeper hailed them from behind. Ellerton cursed softly. "The ostler must have told him," he said to Susan.

"Sir," repeated the innkeeper, bustling forward to them. "Should you be up and about? It seems a mite soon to be—"

"I'm taking him for a drive," interrupted Susan in her customary positive tone. "He needs fresh air."

The man looked doubtful.

"The doctor thinks it will be good for me," added Ellerton, silently apologizing for the lie. He liked the landlord.

"Ah. The doctor does." He nodded wisely. "That's all right, then. But I hope you won't be late, my lord. I've found a brace of partridges for your dinner."

For the first time, Ellerton realized that he would not be coming back to the inn. He would not make the journey twice, but would go on to his own London house. He had not considered the aftermath of his errand until now. And it seemed ungrateful to go off this way without a word. He glanced up at the inn. All here had been very kind.

"Is your leg hurting you?" asked Susan in a pointed tone, as if to remind him that they risked further discovery standing here.

"Lord, yes, I shouldn't keep you on your feet," exclaimed the innkeeper. "Have a pleasant drive." And raising a hand in farewell, he turned away.

"Come on!" added Susan.

The baron allowed her to urge him to the chaise. If his purpose were not so important, he thought, then shook off this hesitation. It *was* important, important enough to risk his own health. He could not be deterred by politeness.

"Can you climb up?" said Susan.

Ellerton looked at the chaise steps. "I shall have to," he replied.

But at that moment, the landlord reappeared with two of the ostlers behind him. "I don't know what I was thinking of," he said, and Susan and the baron froze. "You'll never get up into that carriage alone. Jem and Bill here will lift you."

Susan let out her breath. Ellerton nodded. "Thank you."

At last they were both inside, and Susan leaned out to signal the driver. Ellerton, his injured leg propped up on the seat opposite and swathed in blankets and cushions, still couldn't help wincing a little as they started off, but the first jerk was succeeded by a smoother movement, and he decided the bouncing would not be too bad.

"I've told him to go slowly and carefully," said Susan.

"Thank you." Ellerton sat back and let himself relax, for the first time at leisure to examine his surroundings. His eye fell on a basket in the opposite corner. "Is that . . . you haven't brought that hellish cat, have you?"

As if in answer, the lid of the basket popped up and Daisy's ginger-furred head appeared. He focused gleefully malevolent yellow eyes directly on the baron.

Ellerton groaned.

"Daisy is under strict orders to be good," said Susan, fixing the cat with an admonitory glance. "But he hates being shut in the house all the time, you know."

"I do not understand," answered Ellerton, "why someone, most likely your parents, has not strangled you ere this. To bring that animal, after all that has passed, it is . . ." He stopped, for once at a loss for words.

"He won't bother you," retorted Susan. "And I don't think you should speak to me so when I am *helping* you."

The baron looked at her, and she grimaced. He put his head back on the seat cushions and closed his eyes.

There was a silence. Daisy could be heard emerging from his basket and establishing himself on the plush seat.

"You haven't told me why you must be in London," Susan said then.

Ellerton opened his eyes. "And I don't intend to."

"I should think that after all I have done—"

"You would be mistaken." His tone was extremely discouraging, but Susan merely frowned and bit her lower lip in thought. Another silence fell, in which could be heard a peculiar rasping noise. "I hope you are prepared to pay for the upholstery," added Ellerton. "Your cat is destroying it."

"Daisy!" Susan leaned forward and disengaged his claws from the plush. Holding them in one hand and shaking a warning finger, she said, "You will be shut in your basket if you do not stop it."

With every appearance of sullen rebellion, the cat subsided onto the seat. The baron suppressed a smile.

"Where are we to take you?" asked Susan then, her voice carefully casual. "Your house?"

Ellerton went very still, cursing himself for having overlooked this detail. He had to go directly to the Goring house to find Georgina, yet how could he explain this to Susan without revealing his purpose, which he absolutely refused to do. He could not even leave the girl and go on, for she lived at his destination.

Susan was gazing curiously at him.

"You will see when we arrive," he responded curtly. "Now please be silent. I slept poorly, and I should like to try to make it up while we drive."

She obeyed, but she also smiled at her triumph over him. Where they were going would tell her a great deal about his goal, she concluded. For Susan had no intention of ending this adventure without discovering what that might be.

Ellerton did not really expect to sleep, and he did not, though he kept his eyes closed to discourage Susan from talking. Indeed, his impatience built with every tedious mile, and he longed to command the driver to whip up his horses and return to town at the breakneck pace he had left it on that ill-omened drive that now seemed so long ago. But his leg made that impossible, and he had to endure the whole journey at a near-walk. He tried to pass the time by thinking of what he would say to Georgina, but this merely intensified his frustration, and he came close to anger at her for leaving him in the first place before he caught himself, remembering that it was his own fault.

Finally, after what seemed an age, Susan said, "We are in town now. Where am I to direct the coachman?"

The issue could no longer be avoided. Ellerton faced it squarely. "Your grandmother's house."

She gaped at him. This was not what she had expected. "Our house? But why?"

Ellerton braced himself mentally. "It is very important that I speak to your cousin. She left before I could do so."

"But Georgina was at the inn for days." Susan was frowning at the floor, trying to work this out.

"Nonetheless. Will you tell the man?"

Starting, Susan leaned out and gave the directions; then she turned back to gaze at him. "This doesn't have anything to do with me, does it?"

"Nothing whatsoever," he assured her cordially.

She abandoned her notion that he might be going to complain of her conduct to her grandmother. It had not been a satisfying theory in any case. "Why did you not write Georgina a letter?" she asked.

"I wished to speak to her," he answered, wishing fervently that the driver would go a bit faster. Only their arrival would silence her, he knew.

Susan frowned at the floor once again. She could not imagine what important matter Ellerton would have to discuss with Georgina.

It was at this moment that the baron was visited by inspiration. His crutches had been laid across the two seats in the middle of the carriage, where it was widest, and the tips rested very close to where Daisy curled. Glancing quickly at Susan, and seeing that she was wrapped up in her thoughts, Ellerton grinned wickedly and took hold of one crutch, unobtrusively poking Daisy sharply in the side. In the next instant, his hand was withdrawn and he was gazing innocently out the chaise window.

Daisy reacted predictably to this insult. He sprang

up and glared all around. Then, the absence of visible foes not deterring him in the least, he leapt across the vehicle to fasten his claws in the plush covering the wall between the two passengers' heads. Yellow eyes glittering, he hung there, plotting his next move.

"Daisy!" cried Susan.

"Watch it," exclaimed Ellerton at the same moment, for the cat had leapt again, coming perilously close to landing on his injured leg.

From that point, chaos reigned. Daisy jumped from one wall to another, eluding their furious grabs with apparent ease. Despite a number of close calls, he never hurtled out the open windows or fell to the floor, but he did jar the baron's leg more than once, eliciting a groan and clenched teeth, along with a conviction that he had made a mistake in provoking the animal.

At last Susan managed to throw both arms around the cat and hamper his movements with her skirts. Ellerton thought she would be scratched to ribbons, but to his surprise, Daisy did not touch her. In fact, he allowed himself to be scolded soundly and stuffed back into his basket, the lid securely fastened over his head. That accomplished, Susan sank back and let out a sigh of relief. Both of them were panting from the battle.

"He doesn't scratch you?" asked the baron curiously.

"Oh, no."

"But why not?"

The girl seemed surprised. "He wouldn't."

"I can't imagine that there is anything that beast 'wouldn't' do."

Susan seemed almost shocked. "He would never

hurt *me*. We love each other." She paused, then added, "We are very much alike, you see."

That Susan should echo a conclusion he himself had reached surprised Ellerton again. He looked at her with new interest.

But Susan had already dismissed the subject from her mind. "Are you going to tell me what you wish to speak to Georgina about?" she asked flatly.

"No," he replied with equal bluntness.

"I think it is very unkind of you, after I have helped you this way."

"I would not have required help, if it had not been for your earlier antics."

This was unanswerable. Susan scowled and turned toward the window. "Here we are."

The chaise was indeed drawing up before Lady Goring's house. Ellerton saw with relief that the street was empty. He hoped to make this visit quietly, though of course Lady Goring's servants must inevitably know of it.

"Fetch some of your grandmother's footmen," he said to Susan when they had come to a stop. "I fear I cannot climb down." The jolting of the ride had made his leg feel tender and tired.

Susan met his eyes. "What if I won't?"

"I beg your pardon?"

"What if I won't get them—unless you tell me what you are doing here?" Her green eyes glinted.

"Then you would be very sorry indeed," replied Ellerton in an ominously quiet voice.

Susan hesitated, then wrinkled her nose. "Oh, very well!" And catching up Daisy's basket, she jumped out of the carriage. The baron let out a long sigh. He had had no idea what he would do if she balked.

In a few minutes, Susan reappeared with help,

and Ellerton was gently lowered from the chaise and escorted into the library just off the front hall. At his signal, Susan dismissed the servants. He thought she might make another attempt to pressure him when he asked her to fetch Georgina, but she did not, and shortly thereafter Ellerton heard steps approaching down the stairs and Georgina herself appeared in the doorway.

"Baron Ellerton! What are you doing here? You should not have—"

"I had to speak to you," he broke in. "Please come in and shut the door."

Astonished, she obeyed, and outside in the hall, a slender red-haired girl slipped down the stairs and applied her ear to the door panels.

18

By the time she had taken a seat opposite him, Georgina had somewhat recovered from her amazement. "You were not to travel," she said. "Oh, I hope you have not hurt your leg. The doctor said—"

"It couldn't be helped," interrupted the baron again. "It was imperative I speak to you."

"To *me*?"

"Yes." He had pondered his beginning, and he was prepared, indeed eager, to press ahead. "You left the inn abruptly." She started to protest, and he held up a hand. "At my, er, instigation, I admit. Do you know why I spoke to you in that way about going?"

Georgina shook her head. Something in his voice had made her heart begin to pound, and she was not certain she could speak out loud.

"I was angry. You had said the previous afternoon that you were going, without a hint to me of your intentions, and that made me very angry." He paused. "Because I did not wish you to go, you see."

"I . . . I never meant to, really," breathed Georgina.

"No?" His eyes were fixed on her face.

"No, I just . . . that is . . ." She could not explain her feelings and doubts to him. "I knew I would have to go eventually. I didn't *want* to."

Ellerton had seen what he hoped for in her expression. "Neither of us wanted it, then," he replied. "And why was that, I wonder?"

The teasing note brought Georgina's eyes to his again. She saw there everything she had wished for, and despaired of. Unexpectedly, she smiled. "Perhaps because we enjoyed each other's company."

"Far more than that." He did not smile yet. "I love you, Georgina. I realized that when you had gone. Will you be my wife?"

"Yes," she answered, and felt as if a great bubble of joy had burst in her chest.

"Damn this leg!" exclaimed the baron savagely, making Georgina start. "I cannot get up, you know." His mouth twisted. "Will you come here?"

She rose and went to kneel beside his armchair, on the side away from the footstool where his leg was propped. Her smile reappeared.

But Ellerton's joy in her acceptance was lost in frustration over his state. To be unable to move, to take the woman he loved in his arms, was intolerable. He felt both enraged and humiliated. "Damn!" he said again.

Georgina did not ask him what was wrong. She knew, and knew too that speaking of it would merely make it worse. Instead, she leaned a little forward and slid her arms around his neck, bringing her face very close to his. Then, tentatively, she kissed him.

It was not an expert kiss. Georgina had had no experience in such matters, and she was, in spite of her insight, a bit unsure of herself. But it was enough. Ellerton's arms tightened around her, pulling her into the chair with him, and he kissed her in turn, teaching Georgina more about the subject in a moment than she had gleaned in twenty-nine years. Elated, she gave herself up to his embrace.

Somehow, the awkwardness disappeared. Georgina's feet came to rest beside his leg on the footstool, and she rested against the length of his body in the wide chair, arms entwined about his neck. Ellerton's hands roamed at first gently, then more urgently along her back, firing Georgina with feelings she had never imagined. It was as if all they had felt for one another, misunderstood and thwarted till now, burst out to submerge them in passion.

When at last they drew a little apart, both were panting and a bit taken aback by the violence of their feelings. They simply gazed for a long moment; then Ellerton laughed shakily. "You know, my one concern was that we were too much friends to feel great passion. Clearly, I was mistaken."

She nodded, still breathless.

"And I have never in my life been so happy to be wrong," he added, smiling down at her.

Georgina nodded again.

"Have you nothing to say?"

"I love you," she murmured. "I . . . I am so happy, I don't know what else to say."

This, evidently, sufficed, for Ellerton bent to kiss her once again, and they were oblivious of all else for a prolonged period.

"Perhaps we should, rather, be thankful for my accident," he said after a while. "I don't think I could answer for my restraint otherwise."

"*I'm* not thankful," declared Georgina. Her pale blond hair had come loose from the knot on top of her head and was curling about her face. With her color heightened by emotion, she was achingly beautiful.

He laughed. "Then I am!"

Georgina made a face at him, and raised her lips to kiss him, showing the great strides she had made in this endeavor in only twenty minutes. His hands slid caressingly along her sides, and she shivered with pleasure.

But Ellerton drew away first. "You really must sit here," he said, indicating the chair arm. "What has become of the quiet, steady woman who nursed me through my injuries?"

Georgina grinned. "I believe you have swept her completely away." She offered her lips once more, but he looked stern and pointed to the chair arm. Still smiling, Georgina extricated herself and perched on it.

He took her hand. "The change really is, er, startling."

She shrugged. "You have only yourself to blame." Then, more seriously, she added, "And it is not such a change, I think. One can know nothing of another's feelings until one comes close. I suppose many of our acquaintances feel things we don't imagine, because we don't know them well enough."

"I will not admit they are as extraordinary as you," he responded.

She bent to kiss him. Somehow, though neither knew how, Georgina resumed her previous place in the chair, and they forgot all else once more. Then she moved an arm unexpectedly and jarred his injured ribs, eliciting a quickly stifled groan. In an instant she was up and sitting on the arm again. "Your ribs, I forgot!"

"It's nothing. I'm all right." Some of his chagrin had returned. "One feels damnably ridiculous trying to make love from an armchair."

"You could never be ridiculous," she objected.

The sound of the bell made them both stiffen. Then Georgina said, "They won't bring anyone here. Gibbs will take them to the drawing room and inquire."

But in the hall, Susan scowled. She had been able to hear enough to utterly fascinate her, and the interruption was infuriating. Yet she did not wish to be discovered by the servants in her present position. Grimacing, she dashed to the front door and flung it open.

Tony Brinmore stood on the step, considerably startled by the violence of his welcome and the presence of Susan rather than a footman. He opened his mouth to speak, but she gestured him in and whirled.

Mystified, Tony entered, closing the door behind him. Susan had returned to her post. "What are you—?"

"Shhh!"

Frowning, he took a step closer. "What are you doing?" he whispered.

"Baron Ellerton is proposing to Georgina," she hissed.

"Nonsense."

"Shhh!"

"You must have got it wrong," he murmured. "No sign of that when we were out—"

"Listen for yourself," whispered Susan. "And do be quiet!"

Unhesitatingly Tony joined her. From within, he dimly heard Baron Ellerton say, "When shall we be married?" and Georgina's voice reply, "Before William and Marianne, I think. We mustn't interfere with their plans."

"Well, by Jove," exclaimed Tony.

"Shhh!" said Susan again, exasperated.

They resumed listening, but there were indications now that Georgina was about to emerge. Susan jerked upright. "Come on," she hissed. "In here." And she dragged Tony further down the hall and into the back parlor. They stood silent for a moment, listening, and heard Georgina walking upstairs.

"Well, what do you know about that?" said Tony then. "I never suspected it, did you?"

Susan looked scornful. "Of course."

"You never said anything," he retorted skeptically.

"I'm not a gossip!"

He gaped at her, but decided not to contradict. "We've had a regular rash of offers hereabouts lately," he said instead.

She nodded thoughtfully.

Tony was struck by a sudden idea. Without thinking, he said, "Maybe you and I should join in, eh?" The moment the words were out of his mouth, he regretted them. Indeed, he was aghast. He began to stammer a disjointed retraction.

"Are you mad?" said Susan. "Marry you? I wouldn't dream of it."

Weak with relief, he agreed with her. "Terrible idea. I believe I *was* mad. Must have been."

"Come on," said Susan disgustedly. "Let's go and twit Baron Ellerton on his engagement. He will be sorry he wouldn't tell me what he meant to do." She grinned wickedly. "And I must remind him that he is to be my cousin now."

Tony, who would have gladly followed her anywhere short of the altar at that moment, walked behind her into the hall.

About the Author

Jane Ashford grew up in the American Midwest. A lifelong love of English literature led her eventually to a doctorate in English, and to extensive travel in England. After working as a teacher and an editor, she began to write, drawing on her knowledge of eighteenth and nineteenth century history. She is also very fond of cats. She now divides her time between New York City and Lakeville, Connecticut.

More Regency Romances from SIGNET